Julia sat on the roof's edge, feet crossed, watching as locals streamed into that Burger King. Rules dictated that she wait until no one was around, so that she wouldn't be seen, which was one reason why she chose the health club's roof. But if she waited much longer, she'd eat shingles.

A guy with a huge rig filled with all kinds of snow-moving equipment parked in the auxiliary parking lot, as far from anyone as he could get. He climbed out of his four-by-four, pushed the hood of a parka off his head, and wiped his face.

He had beautiful black hair in need of a trim. He was tall and broad-shouldered, and moved with the ease of an athlete. He didn't look up as he walked, and she felt oddly disappointed.

She wanted to see his face.

The Santa Series

READING ORDER

THE SANTA SERIES

Up on the Rooftop

Visions of Sugar Plums

Dressed in Holiday Style

Tidings of Comfort and Joy

Santa Claus Lane

All the books in The Santa Series *standalone and can be read out of order. However, some books have characters from the previous stories in them.*

Also by Kristine Grayson

THE FATES UNIVERSE

The Fates Trilogy

Simply Irresistible

Absolutely Captivated

Totally Spellbound

The Daughters of Zeus Trilogy

Tiffany Tumbles

Crystal Caves

Brittany Bends

Other Books in the Fates Universe

Completely Smitten

The Charming Trilogy, Vol. 1

The Charming Trilogy, Vol. 2

THE RETRIEVAL ARTIST SERIES

A Murder of Clones

Search & Recovery

The Peyti Crisis

Vigilantes

Starbase Human

Masterminds

The Impossibles

The Retrieval Artist

Writing as Kris Nelscott

THE SMOKEY DALTON SERIES

A Dangerous Road

Smoke-Filled Rooms

Thin Walls

Stone Cribs

War at Home

Days of Rage

Street Justice

Up On The Rooftop

THE SANTA SERIES

KRISTINE GRAYSON

WMG
PUBLISHING

Up On The Rooftop

JULKA STOOD ON the roof, hands on her hips, feet covered in snow. She was tired, she was cold, and she hadn't felt the tip of her nose in hours. She was staring at yet another fancy-pants chimney, a narrow little pipe sticking up out of a lovely square pile of fake bricks, and she wanted to kick it.

Which wasn't very festive of her.

But seriously, who felt festive on October 30th? It was New England, for heavens sake. There wasn't supposed to be snow for another—oh, what? Two weeks? She really didn't know, except that she had checked the records going back to the 19th century, and never found a snowfall as deep as this one *before* Halloween. She wasn't supposed to be this cold for another month, and by then, she should've been moving south. Where she would have to deal with freezing fog, sleet, and sheets of ice.

Oh, joy. Ho-ho-ho and all that.

It was her own damn fault that she was standing here. She was the one who had said, *I don't have the skills to run a workshop, but I can find problems and solve them.*

And then, of course, she had to go too far, because she always went too far: *Besides, I don't want to stay here for my entire life. I'd like to travel. I need to see the world. I really, really do.*

She sighed. When she had said she wanted to see the world, she had hoped she would be placed in one of the many year-round outposts. She would receive toy shipments, interview local children, and make certain that the back-up sleighs were in fantastic shape. She would scout local products and find great toy factories that didn't even know they would be enlisted.

She had wanted to be one of the Ambassadors for Santa's massive worldwide operation.

She hadn't meant that she wanted to be a minion in Entry Access Quality Control, someone who had to view each and every house with children in it for the appropriate entrance. Appropriate, in Santa's rather medieval mind, always meant a chimney.

She sighed and clutched the tablet to her chest. It was a real paper tablet—one of the millions of Big Chief tablets that someone in Santa's North Pole headquarters had stocked up on in the 1960s, along with stubby Number 2 pencils that she refused to use.

She wanted an electronic tablet—a gizmo, with bells and whistles and access to the worldwide web (even though, she'd been told, no one called it that any more). The workshop had hundreds of those as well, but not for the elves or the human support staff, but for the tech-savvy children who didn't want a dolly or a train set, but who wanted the latest in computer gadgetry.

Everyone at the North Pole had to be careful with gadgetry. Many types of magic—particularly fairy tale magic—weren't compatible with electronics. Elven magic also had difficulty with electronics. Santa always had the Fairy Kingdoms design his systems, and that didn't always work well.

Delbert popped his head out of the invisible sleigh. She hated the effect. It made him look like he'd been beheaded, and she had gotten stuck with the head part. She wondered what the civilians on the ground saw. Whatever it was, it couldn't've been pretty.

Entry Access Quality Control wasn't supposed to call attention to itself. That was why the invisible sleigh, which was the same size and shape as Santa's (only without the reindeer; they hadn't needed reindeer since 1930 or so, but they kept the reindeer for form's sake. Besides, the reindeer had a hell of a union).

Delbert usually remained invisible as well. He was an S-Elf, sharing a lineage with Santa. Delbert hated his heritage, and would've fled long ago except that he couldn't hide who he was, no matter how much he wanted to. All those photos of Santa vacationing on the beach, of Santa in Hawaii in the summer or lounging in Monte Carlo instead of driving his sleigh—well, they weren't Santa.

They were usually Delbert.

And as punishment for tarnishing the Santa brand, he had to spend one year on Entry Access Quality Control.

"Well," Delbert said, "do I have to put my boots on?"

"No," Julka said sourly. He might have been punished by doing Entry Access Quality Control, but she was the one who suffered. She inspected, kicked, shook, and fought with more chimneys than she wanted to consider. Yes, she had the best boots and gloves that magic could conjure, but she still got cold and wet and *grumpy*.

Delbert only had to emerge when there was a likely chimney, which there hadn't been all day.

The rules of Entry Access Quality Control were pretty simple: if the chimney didn't work, and the skylight looked too dicey, then Santa got to use any available door. And Delbert didn't have to check the doors. With the growing obesity problem worldwide, the entire slew of Santa Advance Teams no longer had to worry about doorways being too narrow for the Jolly Old Elf.

"I'll boil up some lunch then," Delbert said. "You gonna want any?"

"No, thanks." She couldn't stomach a second day of

Peppermint Veal Stew, even if the elves did think it a delicacy. Her stomach didn't. Neither did her taste buds. That was the other problem of traveling with elves. They preferred sweet foods to almost everything else, turning the most disgusting things into candy.

She'd grown up with it, but that didn't mean she liked it. After the last few days, she deserved something made here in the Greater World, not that it was greater than the North Pole's magical universe. The Greater World was just bigger—and lacked the magic.

Which she was really beginning to appreciate.

Because magic—what little of it she had—was making her cold.

M ARSHALL COLLIER SHADED his eyes with his right hand, and looked up at the roof. It wasn't a trick of the light. He was seeing a slight figure holding some kind of notebook kick a chimney. Tiny runnels of snow trickled down the side of the rooftop, like the precursors of an avalanche.

Or at least, a severe loss of roof-snow that would ruin the shoveling work he had managed earlier this morning.

Marshall had a narrow flatbed truck that could hold a small Caterpillar tractor with a large shovel on the end, and two different size snow blowers. He also had real honest-to-God shovels tucked into the back and three changes of clothing, including pairs of boots.

He'd been out clearing side streets and sidewalks since 5 a.m, calling the power company every two blocks or so to report downed lines, and doing his best to be a Good Samaritan.

This freak pre-Halloween blizzard, and his parka, had given him a kind of anonymity that he hadn't had since the Great Recession began. It hadn't mattered that he hadn't worked for the fraudulent companies that caused the meltdown. What mattered was that he had made a lot of money (too much money) as an investment banker and venture capitalist. It also didn't matter that he had retired from that business in 2007 at the age of 34. What seemed to matter to all these folks who were struggling to pay their now-overpriced mortgages on their meager unemployment benefits, was that he had once worked in that industry, and that meant he was one step above Satan.

And maybe he was. When he worked in the industry, he hadn't thought that there were actual people behind the numbers. He wasn't a sales guy. He had been an analysis guy. He hadn't dealt with people; he had dealt with numbers.

As the economy tumbled into darker and darker places, he had watched the news reports with horror, realizing that each number he had played with had represented someone else's money.

The thing was, he hadn't been told that when he was hired straight out of Harvard. No one said a word as he had manipulated the numbers, stroked and fondled them and made them grow—legitimately—until the returns he got weren't good enough for his bosses. They wanted him to cheat on the math. He never cheated on anything. Not on tests, not on girlfriends, and certainly not on something as important as his job.

So he got fired for not taking enough risks. But he had already taken a big risk: he had put some of his earnings into a buddy's company. The company looked dicey from the beginning, but a friend was a friend, right? He had then invested in a few other companies, calling himself a venture capitalist, when really he was a depressed fired former investment banker.

And then his buddy's company became a huge success. And Marshall, as one of the early investors, made a fortune.

He pulled out of the venture capital business because he didn't want to make his fortune into an obscene fortune, especially not while his neighbors were starving. So he concentrated his efforts on helping charities become more efficient—manipulating numbers again, but for a good cause. (And giving away money.)

But he never talked about any of that, and everyone in this rather toney neighborhood thought of him as that investment banker guy. Hated, as if he had robbed all those funds all by himself.

He had no idea why he kept trying to ingratiate himself with the people in this place, but he did. He kept telling himself it was because he liked his house and he didn't want to move—which was true—but honestly, it might've been because he was trying to ingratiate himself with himself. He had let himself become part of the problem, and he really hadn't tried to implement a solution, back when there could have been one.

Guilt. It went a long way. Including getting him out at 5 a.m. on a blizzardy morning, clearing roads and driveways for people who would spit on him if they knew he was the one behind the wheel of the snow blower.

Still, six hours of work later, he was feeling pretty good. He wasn't cold, he wasn't wet, and he had managed to clear miles of roadway and driveway by his own rather mighty self.

Sometimes good physical labor felt a lot better than massaging numbers. Even if that meant he was seeing the same people over and over again on rooftops.

Although that wasn't really accurate. He was seeing the same *person* over and over again on rooftops. She was tiny, slender, and stylish, wearing a little red cape with fur trim. (He hoped it was fake fur trim. In this neighborhood, wearing fur could get her killed.) She also had on reddish pants tucked into knee-high boots. She was wearing fur earmuffs and no gloves at all. And she looked cold.

When he had first seen her, he thought she was a child. She was so slim and so regal, and her outfit so outlandish for someone going from roof to roof, that he figured she had to be about twelve. A few houses ago, he had gotten closer, and realized if she was twelve, she should've been locked inside the house.

She had a curvy figure appropriate to her small size, and golden blond hair that he hadn't seen outside of shampoo commercials. He couldn't quite see her face, but her body language wasn't twelve either. It was exasperated adult—or it had been, until she gave the chimney in front of her one frustrated kick.

He frowned at her. He had no idea why a woman dressed like she was heading for a Macy's Christmas photo shoot would travel from rooftop to rooftop in a MacMansion-filled Connecticut neighborhood. Nor did he know exactly how she was doing it. Or what angered her about it so much.

He did know that he found her fascinating, from the tip of her golden hair to her impractical boots. He wondered if he should yell up at her and warn her that too many sudden movements would cause the snow to slide off the roof—and her with it.

Then she stomped away from him, toward the back of the house. She reached the peak of the roof, stepped up some kind of ladder that he couldn't see—and vanished.

And not a wink-out disappear complete with little sparklies. Nor was it like a transporter vanish in *Star Trek* where the entire body fuzzed into a multicolored light show. It was as if she got swallowed by something. First her head and shoulders disappeared, along with one of her feet and an arm, then her torso, and finally the remaining foot. All that remained was a disturbance in the Force (as Obi-Wan would have said), which looked rather like a heat mirage, floating briefly next to that chimney.

Then nothing. Nothing at all. Not even the house next door. At least, not for a few seconds, anyway. It was as if someone had set up an opaque wall, designed to match the snow and the gray cloud cover (which was threatening even more ugliness).

He blinked and the neighbor's rooftop reappeared. And so did a few more rooftops he hadn't known were missing.

Okay, that was it. Six hours of physical labor in the cold, moving tractors and snow blowers and piles of snow, subsisting on stale (lukewarm) coffee, breakfast bars, and one apple, had not done him any good.

It was time to take a break. It was past time to take a break.

He sighed, rubbed his eyes, and headed to lunch.

THE
Santa
SERIES

IT HAD TAKEN Julka fifteen minutes to convince Delbert that she needed to stop at the Burger King two miles away. He just wanted to go to the next rooftop. He had some vision of getting done before nightfall. Like that was going to happen. They wouldn't be done until the morning of December 23rd. Although to be fair, he was only referring to this town, and in this town they only had 35 houses left to go.

Besides, they had already earned hotel money. Julka liked that best of all. The teams that couldn't get their quotas done in the time allotted had to sleep in their sleighs. But Julka and Delbert were one day ahead of schedule, partly because of the blizzard. They'd worked around it, using the North Pole Navigator to let them know when and where the worst of the weather would be. Then they would go to the safest part of their region, get the work done, and move onto another area, avoiding most of the snow the entire time.

The Burger King's roof had been shoveled off. It had a single pipe that spewed smoke that smelled of frying beef. A gigantic Halloween pumpkin balloon had been shredded by the blizzard's middle-of-the-night winds and hung off the roof like orange streamers. Since reddish orange was one of Burger King's primary colors, the streamers looked planned.

Nothing else did. The parking lot was jammed. Julka had to convince Delbert to land on the nearby health club's roof. She had hoped to land in the parking lot.

But the parking lot—which was huge—was also full.

She sat on the roof's edge, feet crossed, watching as locals streamed into that Burger King. Rules dictated that she wait until no one was around, so that she wouldn't be seen, which was one reason why she chose the health club's roof. But if she waited much longer, she'd eat shingles.

A guy with a huge rig filled with all kinds of snow-moving equipment parked in the auxiliary parking lot, as far from anyone as he could get. He climbed out of his four-by-four, pushed the hood of a parka off his head, and wiped his face.

He had beautiful black hair in need of a trim. He was

tall and broad-shouldered, and moved with the ease of an athlete. He didn't look up as he walked, and she felt oddly disappointed. She wanted to see his face.

She had a feeling she'd seen him before, but she had no idea where.

She lost sight of him in the scrum of vehicles in the main parking lot. He had been the last non-magical person in her line of vision. She grinned, then launched herself off the roof.

Jumping from rooftops had not been one of her magical skills until she took this job. Then she got an augmentation just so she was protected from accidental slippage or falls of more than three feet. This was the best perk of all—that feeling of floating through a cushion of air. It made her feel like she could fly if she would only put her mind to it.

She landed on the sidewalk outside the health club. She adjusted her hair and her ear muffs, hoping she looked enough like a regular person—a regular American person—to get by.

This was the one thing she had little experience with, the one thing she valued the most: the opportunity to mingle with regular people, the kind the Pole was designed to help. She knew she could never quite blend in, but she could at least experience everything like the tourist she was, making memories, snatching moments out of other people's every day lives and wondering what she would have been like if she had been born in New England instead of the North Pole.

She squared her shoulders, adjusted her cape, and headed for the front door.

THE
Santa
SERIES

NORMALLY, MARSHALL WAS a "my-body-is-my-temple" kinda guy. He watched what he ate, exercised regularly, and got enough sleep. After six hours of intensive labor in the frigid cold, he figured it wasn't going to hurt him to eat poorly.

And he was planning to eat very poorly.

He pulled into Burger King like it was the holy of holies. He looked at that cheesy sign he usually drove past (with his head down so he didn't have to contemplate all that burgery goodness) and reveled in the idea of a Whopper or a bacon-double cheeseburger or maybe both, along with fifteen sides of fries, and eighteen regular Cokes.

He'd spend his afternoon in the plastic seats, leaning

against a faux marble table, and watching the neighborhood go by. His neighbors would shun him and treat him badly and he would have to hide behind the pieces of *The New York Times* someone had carelessly left lying about.

That thought—and not the fifteen orders of fries—nearly had him swerving for the drive-through.

But he hadn't. He had forced himself to go inside.

He had never seen the Burger King so busy. People lined up five deep. Entire families huddled together, looking miserable. It wasn't until he eavesdropped that he understood why.

Many houses in the neighborhood had no power. Burger King was the closest fast-food restaurant—any restaurant, really—with electricity. A woman behind the counter grinned tiredly at one customer, and said, "We've been like this all morning."

Startled, Marshall looked at the clock. It *was* morning to most people. His day was half done. More than half done, really. And now that he had stopped moving, he was done in.

No wonder he'd been seeing pretty girl elves on rooftops. He was half asleep on his feet.

He ordered a Double Whopper with large fries and both Coke and coffee—the coffee for warmth.

Lucky him, he found an open table that fit two, so he didn't feel like he was taking spots away from cold families. Everyone sounded miserable. Kids asking if they could trick or treat when the power was out; parents giving the time-honored "we'll see" response that probably meant no. If power lines were still down, then no one was wandering neighborhoods in costume any time soon, and he doubted that anyone would have the time or the ability to set up a one-stop trick-or-treat place.

He'd never seen anything quite like it: this full blizzard so early in the season, wrecking so many plans.

"I'd blame you for this, except I, at least, know you're not God," said one of his neighbors, Hester Bain, as she walked by Marshall with her ten-year-old son, Nigel.

Nigel gave Marshall an apologetic glance. Marshall shrugged. Hester Bain ("That's Mrs. Bain to you") had been vicious to him from the moment she found out who he had been, at a neighborhood meeting from late 2008 that he still regretted—not that he went to the meeting, but that he had said, "I know a lot of those guys—I used to work in the industry—and believe me, most of them don't have souls."

Apparently "most of them" had applied to him too. He tried to shrug moments like this off—after all, the Bains had lost all of their life savings with one of the scam investment houses, and they had barely managed to hang onto their house—but the words still hurt.

He made himself look away from her. He didn't want to meet anyone's gaze. He didn't want to provoke more comments.

Then a flash of red caught his eye. He turned toward the door, and his breath caught.

There she was: taller than he had initially thought, older too—maybe 30—with a face as stunning as her wheat-blond hair. High cheekbones, blue eyes, delicate lips—she looked like a Russian supermodel.

She also looked stunningly out of place. It wasn't just her red cape with the fur trim and matching red pants tucked into those black leather boots. It was the happy expression on her face.

Everyone else was miserable, a bit frightened, worried about the weather and the future, and she smiled like she had entered the happiest place on Earth.

Plus it was the day before Halloween, and she looked like Santa's Naughty Helper before the half-naked photo shoot started.

His cheeks warmed, and he forced himself to look away. He normally didn't think of women like that, not even exceedingly pretty women. Not even exceedingly pretty women whom he found exceedingly attractive.

He could feel her nearby. He wondered if she was staring at him, then decided that he was just being silly. She hadn't noticed him at all. In fact, if she was from the neighborhood, she probably knew what an awful person he was supposed to be and would most certainly avoid him.

At least she hadn't been a figment of his imagination. Although that begged the question—what had she been doing on that rooftop?

Those rooftops, if he really wanted to be accurate.

He wanted to get up and ask her. He wondered how creepy that would be. Would she think he was spying on her or something?

"Pardon me," a low female voice with an odd accent asked him.

He lifted his head, and there she was, large as life and much more fragrant. She smelled peppermint, which somehow didn't surprise him one bit.

"Is this seat taken?" she asked softly. "It seems to be the only one available."

"Um, sure," he said. "I mean, no. I mean, please, sit down."

When was the last time a woman had him tongue-tied? When was the last time he had spoken to an attractive woman? He broke up with his most recent girlfriend a year ago, he didn't go to bars to meet women, and no one in town wanted anything to do with him. He would have had to take a train into New York City just to find a woman who didn't mind his background.

The pretty woman smiled at him, and the entire room brightened. He was surprised that no one else seemed to notice.

"Thank you," she said and slipped into the hard plastic chair, setting her tray down as she did. "I have wanted to come here for a long time."

To Connecticut? To Burger King? To *this* Burger King? He knew she hadn't meant the table or the spot near the window.

"I take it you're not local," he said, and silently cursed himself for being idiotic.

"Sadly, no," she said. "I am only in your fair city for a few days for work. Then I move south."

"Move south?" he asked.

She shrugged one shoulder. "My work requires that I go from place to place."

"And your work is on...rooftops?" he asked.

She looked at him, surprised. "How do you know that?"

"I saw you today," he said. "It's hard to miss you in that red cape."

She looked down at herself as if she just realized what she was wearing. "Is it inappropriate?"

"I don't know," he said. "It is the day before Halloween. But usually people reserve their elf costumes for Christmas."

"Elf costume?" she said in a decidedly frigid tone.

"Well, you know," Marshall said, his cheeks getting even warmer. "The red cape, the fur, the boots..."

God, he almost blurted that she looked like Santa's Naughty Helper, but he somehow managed to censor that statement. Still, she looked offended.

"I am *not* an elf," she said.

"I-I-I know," he said. "I'm sorry. I didn't mean to insult you. It's a very fetching costume."

He sounded so lame, like some needy geek around a pretty girl. Which he was. Before he had gotten into

Harvard, hell, before he had become an investment banker, long before he had money, he had been the math geek in the corner of the high school cafeteria, lost in his numbers, unable to talk to any girl he found attractive—even if (especially if) she had asked him about her math homework.

"It's not a costume," she said in that same frosty tone. "It's my work outfit."

His face probably matched her suit. He didn't even know how to apologize without making things worse.

"Ah," he said. "It's just unusual to see people in red uniforms standing on rooftops in the lull of a snowstorm."

"Oh," she said, "the storm is over—at least here. It's moving north and east."

She sounded so sure of herself.

"That's not what the weather people say." Marshall had checked his phone twice to see the weather, wondering if his labors this morning had even been worthwhile. The weather experts seemed to believe the blizzard would continue—in one form or another—until November.

"Well, we have much more sophisticated equipment," she said.

"We?" he asked.

She shrugged. "The people I work with. We have fantastic equipment, especially about the weather. We have to."

Because they spent their days on rooftops? He felt confused. "I suppose I can't ask who you work with."

She shook her head. Her sandwich was almost gone, and he hadn't even noticed her eating it. "You wouldn't believe me if I told you."

He flashed on that face he had seen on one of the rooftops—the first one?—the face that looked like a disembodied head. Was that one of her partners? Or was that a trick of the light?

He was about to ask her, when a strident female voice cut into their conversation. "I don't know who you are, young lady, but you look nice."

Marshall and the pretty non-elf woman looked toward the sound. It came from Mrs. Bain, two tables away, her lunch crumpled in front of her, her tray pushed to one side. Nigel had his head down, trying to finish his Whopper Jr.

Mrs. Bain leaned toward them as if she was going to speak confidentially, but she didn't lower her voice at all.

"But," Mrs. Bain continued, "that man is one of those bankers who steals from people. He's not the sort of person you should idly converse with. He's despicable."

"What?" The pretty non-elf woman frowned at Mrs. Bain, then looked at Marshall. "Do you mean him?"

He almost closed his eyes. He didn't want to see the disappointment on her face.

But she didn't look disappointed. Just confused.

"I don't understand all the customs here," she was

saying, "but why would a banker have snow removal equipment on the back of a big truck?"

Marshall's breath caught. She had *seen* that? She had been watching him too?

"He probably repossessed it," Mrs. Bain said with great certainty. "It would be just his style to repossess the equipment when people need it most."

"Mom." Nigel touched his mother's arm. "He's been digging people out all day. That's how we got out of our driveway."

Mrs. Bain gave Nigel an alarmed look. "You let him on our property? You were supposed to shovel."

Nigel bowed his head and grabbed some French fries as if they would save him. His face was as red as Marshall's had been.

"To be fair, Mrs. Bain," Marshall said, "there was too much snow for anyone to handle with a shovel."

"Fair?" she snapped. "Don't you talk to me about fair. Don't you talk to any of us about fair."

Marshall sighed. He knew better. He shouldn't have engaged. He never should have said anything. And now the pretty non-elf woman probably thought he was some kind of monster on top of being a clueless tongue-tied idiot.

"Mom," Nigel said softly, without looking up. His fries were arranged in a neat row on his tray. "You're not being nice."

Mrs. Bain stood, then grabbed her empty tray, and

Nigel's half-full one. "Someday, Nigel, you'll learn that there are people in this world who don't deserve nice."

Marshall would have had to agree with that, but only because he was angry, and he didn't dare say anything. Why had she butted into his life? Why did she want to ruin it?

Oh, yeah, because people like him had ruined hers—and his was the face of the disaster, at least to her. He had to keep reminding himself of that.

"Where I work," the pretty non-elf woman said, "we believe all can be redeemed, if they realize they've been naughty."

It took Marshall a moment to understand what she had said. First, he had heard the word "naughty," and that had conjured the wrong image for him. He didn't need to hear her say the word "naughty," not after he had thought it—twice.

But he got past that (he hoped) and realized that the pretty non-elf woman was defending him. It was such an unusual experience that he didn't know what to say.

"Lie to yourself all you like, honey," Mrs. Bain said. "A man like that will disillusion you fast enough. Come along, Nigel."

Nigel shot Marshall another apologetic look. Marshall nodded as imperceptively as he could, and watched as the two of them stalked off. Well, as Mrs. Bain stalked. Nigel trailed like a lost puppy.

"What did you do to them?" the pretty non-elf woman asked.

So much for defense. Guilty until proven innocent. Actually, guilt by association. Years of association, actually.

He had no idea how to explain any of it, especially to a woman who clearly wasn't from around here. She had been kind. She didn't need to hear about his strange existence.

"It's a long story," he said.

"Well," she said. "I've got some time. I'm ahead of schedule, and now that I'm done with this Whopper thing, I'm going to try something else."

Then she grinned, got up, and headed back to the counter.

He watched her in surprise. He had no idea where she was going to put another entire meal—and he shouldn't be watching her, not like this, not with the word "naughty" still floating around in his brain.

He should do the honorable thing: He should get up and leave. Right now. That way he wouldn't embarrass himself any more and he wouldn't upset the neighbors.

But this was the nicest anyone had been to him in a long time—at least, anyone local.

Only she wasn't local.

And somehow, the job she did had something to do with being nice.

So maybe "nice" was just a reflex for her. Still, it made

him feel better. He hadn't realized how down he had been until the pretty non-elf woman stood up for him.

He sipped his now-cold coffee. Then he realized that the Burger King was quiet. Most of the patrons were staring at him. Most of them recognized him, either from the neighborhood or those ill-advised neighborhood meetings.

If the pretty non-elf woman stayed here for a few days, she would want a good experience. And people wouldn't be nice to her if they thought she was a friend of his.

He put the lid on his coffee so that he wouldn't spill it, and stood up. He needed to leave. Not for him so much, but for her. She didn't need to get sucked into his world, not even for an hour, not in a fast-food restaurant where half the neighborhood had gone for lunch. She had looked so joyful when she had come in here.

He didn't want—even inadvertently—to trample on that joy.

Five

H E WAS CUTE. No, he was better than cute. He was *nice*. And really handsome with that dark hair (which needed just a bit of a trim), a little stubble from his long day, and the redness in his cheeks. She hadn't seen a man with such redness in his cheeks this far from home, and she found that she liked it.

Julka stood at the end of the line, bouncing a little on her feet. She liked him, even if other people didn't seem to. He seemed kind. She had no idea what he had done to that horrible lady. (Then Julka sighed at herself: she wasn't supposed to think of anyone as *horrible*, just unreformed.) And even though he had supposedly treated that lady poorly, he had shoveled her walk, saving her little boy from doing work that might have hurt him.

Because the handsome man was right: anyone with

snow experience knew that too much snow had fallen in a short period of time to get rid of it with a simple shovel. It would take mechanical equipment (for the non-magical humans) or some real magical muscle to get rid of the snow in a timely fashion.

And as she had learned throughout her long years at the North Pole, some snow simply refused to be gotten rid of.

She made herself look at the menu. So many choices. If she had known that there were this many choices in all of the various restaurants in the Greater World, she would have stopped eating Delbert's cooking long ago. She had Greater World money, with more of it appearing as she completed each day's task.

Julka turned toward the table only to see the handsome man get up. His shoulders were hunched forward and he was holding his tray in his left hand. He looked defeated.

Something in that interaction with the horrible woman (to heck with it: that appellation was staying) had really bothered him.

"Don't go," she said, slipping out of her place in line. "I'll buy you a fresh coffee."

He gave her that sad smile of his and shook his head. He came toward her, and said softly, "Look, I'm not the most popular person here, and talking to me might ruin your time in this town. So it's best if we don't—"

"Nonsense," she said. "They already saw us talking.

Whatever damage there was is done. Besides, I have some things to ask you."

His sad smile got sadder.

"No," he said. "It's best if we just part ways now. But thank you for your kindness. It means a lot to me."

Then he bowed his head, and walked out of the Burger King.

She almost hurried after him—she hated seeing anyone that upset—but he had been clear. He didn't think it was good for her to be talking to him.

Which just showed his kindness again.

After he disappeared from view, she rejoined the line. Everyone was staring at her—except for the people who were studiously avoiding her gaze. No one was talking.

"What did he do?" she asked the silver-haired man in the table next to her.

"I'm not sure," the man said, his tone dismissive.

But she wasn't going to let it go. "What do you mean, you're not sure. Everyone is treating him like he's done something awful."

"Well, he did," the man said. "We're just not sure what."

"He was an *investment banker*," said the little old lady at the table across from the man, her tones hushed as if she had called the gentleman Julka had been talking to a sex crimes pervert.

"Isn't that a common job?" Julka asked.

"Not exactly," the woman said. "And he is retired."

"So what is the problem?" Julka asked.

"Well, those bankers," the woman said, "they caused the meltdown."

Meltdown? Oh, the woman meant that financial thing that happened a few years back. Julka had to study it in Advanced Greater World Studies, so that she could converse about it. The "meltdown" had a serious impact on children worldwide, making Santa's services even more necessary, and overwhelmed him with extra work.

"You think he had something to do with that?" Julka asked, referring to her handsome gentleman. How could he have? He seemed so nice.

"They all did, those bankers," the woman said in hushed tones.

"And some of 'em really screwed people," the silver-haired man said. "They took money from everyone, leaving us with nothing."

Julka looked out the door, as if she could still see the gentleman. "So why was he digging people out?"

"He seems to think we'll accept him as a neighbor," another woman said snidely from the back. "But we never will. Him and his ilk, they ruined us."

A bunch of others nodded.

"Can't you forgive him?" Julka asked.

Everyone stared at her as if she had grown a third head.

She shrugged. "I mean, he seems really sorry."

"There are some things in life," said the silver-haired man, "that sorry doesn't solve."

THE
Santa
SERIES

Six

ARSHALL WAS COLD, wet, tired and discouraged. He had promised himself that he wouldn't quit until he'd finished the last of the neighborhood, but as he drove down the one plowed street, he saw orange wooden saw horses on the road, with a hand-made sign that warned of more downed power lines.

Earlier in the day, he would have figured out a way around so that he could finish his self-assigned mission, but this time, he simply didn't want to go on. He wanted to get home, take a warm shower, and forget that the day ever happened.

Part of the problem with his neighbors was his house. It was too big for the neighborhood. It didn't matter that he hadn't built it: he had bought it, back when he was feeling flush—a large Tudor/Colonial blend that actually worked. It sat on a rise overlooking the entire neighborhood, and underneath the house proper was a gigantic garage that originally housed the first owner's antique car collection.

As Marshall rounded the corner, he hit the garage door opener, then wished he hadn't. The driveway was snowed in again. He had cleared it at five a.m., but there had been quite a bit of snow since then, and even more had toppled off the hillside. The garage door was open, but there was no driving inside until he cleared a path.

He pulled into the turn-around in front of the driveway, shut off the engine and rested his head on the steering wheel. He was inclined to chain the equipment to the truck with padlocks and go inside.

But he knew better. Given the way the neighborhood felt about him, someone would damage the equipment, and he would just blame himself for leaving it outside.

He sighed. Today proved one thing. It didn't matter how much he did, how hard he tried or how many times he explained that he had retired *before* the collapse. He would always be a pariah here.

Much as he loved his house—and he really did—he would have to move. He couldn't stay. He needed to find some other nifty house in another nifty neighborhood— and then he had to avoid the neighborhood meetings, or if he went, he would simply say that he was a retired numbers runner. Because, in essence, that was all he had done.

He had run numbers for a bunch of gamblers who had ignored him anyway. They were getting off scott-free, and he was staying here, inadvertently paying for their mistakes.

And missing opportunities with pretty women who wore inappropriate elf costumes at the end of October, women (woman) who had the most enchanting accent and the loveliest blue eyes he had ever seen.

Too bad he had met her under such strange circumstances.

Too bad he would never see her again.

He certainly would have loved to find out exactly who she was.

Seven

S HE SHOULDN'T HAVE let him go. Julka slipped out of the line, and headed for the door. The poor man. Everyone in this strange town blamed him for something they didn't even understand.

No wonder Santa had a policy of staying out of Greater World affairs.

Julka hurried out of the Burger King. More cars were coming in, all of them with families inside, and everyone looking miserable.

She understood how snow could make people miserable—she got tired of it herself, long about May—but she never understood how anyone minded the first snowfall of the year, particularly one as dramatic as this one had been. Yes, it was cold; yes, the wind was harsh; but oh, it was always so beautiful.

That's what these people—all of them—seemed to be missing: The very beauty of living.

She cut across the parking lot, then went to the side of the health club. She only gave a cursory glance around her to make certain no one was watching—these people were so sour that they probably wouldn't accept real magic if they saw it.

Then she crouched, and sprang upward, using all those magical muscles she had gotten when she got this assignment. She floated up to the roof. The sleigh shimmered ever so slightly, its outline only visible up close, and then only as a cutout against the sky.

She stepped inside, and winced at the stench of peppermint. Delbert was standing at the counter in the back, making a chocolate peppermint banana smoothie. She didn't even have to check her watch. The appearance of the smoothie meant it was now officially afternoon.

"Took you long enough," he said.

She ignored that. He said it every single time she came back in the sleigh. Sometimes the statement was accurate, and sometimes it wasn't. This time, it probably was.

She went over the array of cobbled together computer and magical equipment near the guidance system, and took her seat.

"We need to find someone," she said.

Delbert swallowed the smoothie in one long gulp, then wiped the brownish stain off his face. "Not our job," he said—or rather, mumbled. His mouth was still full of smoothie.

She hated the equipment. It looked like three 1950s television sets combined with a steam engine, rope, and a calliope. It had been designed by Santa hundreds of years ago, and modified every century or so. It hadn't gotten this century's modification because the fairies who designed the system were at war, and Santa didn't want to get involved.

The fairies were, so far as she knew, one of the few groups that could easily combine technology and magic. Santa had relied on them for his entire career. Until now.

She put her hands on the screen. She didn't have the magic to do a Santa-time search, where all she had to do was think of the person and end up with the name, address, personal history and current Naughty/Nice ranking. Instead, she had to use the screen as a window into the camera mounted on the sleigh's runners.

"I want this thing airborne," she said.

"Good," Delbert said. "We going back to work?"

"We're ahead of schedule," she reminded him.

"We still have 35 houses to go," he said.

"And five days allotted. We can do 35 houses in a morning."

"What happened out there?" he asked.

"Just get this thing in the air," she said.

He didn't argue. She was nominally in charge, even if

he was an S-Elf. He was an S-Elf on double-secret forever probation, and he would probably never be in charge of anything ever again.

So he moved across the small cockpit to his little chair. Santa's sleigh had gorgeous benches and seats that molded to your frame. The back-up sleighs were utilitarian because they needed room for food storage, sleeping compartments (uncomfortable and *dangerous* sleeping compartments, which was why the advance team had a hotel budget), clothing, and other supplies.

Delbert's hands moved over what looked, to Julka, like a smooth countertop, and the sleigh shuddered. There were only two reasons an S-Elf had to be on a sleigh. The first was to test—as realistically as possible—Santa's entry into the various houses, and the second was to fly the sleighs. Only S-Elves had the encoding (some of the more scientific types said DNA, but others believed it was just a magical quirk) to get the sleighs in the air.

The sleigh wobbled and tumbled, and then righted itself. Delbert had had too much peppermint and was flying impaired. But Julka wasn't going to report him—at least not yet. Because if she did, then they might send a replacement, and she wouldn't be able to get away with... what? She wasn't sure what she was trying to get away with.

She just knew it was something.

She peered in the glass screen, which bubbled outward

just a bit, distorting the images of rooftops, roads, and snow, snow, snow. Crews worked everywhere, repairing power lines or putting up signs telling people to stay away from lines.

No wonder people looked so sad. She hadn't quite realized the extent of the devastation before. The North Pole knew how to deal with snow from September to May; apparently here, in New England, they did not.

Then she saw what she was looking for: a flatbed truck with snow equipment. It was parked on a road in front of a house, and there he was, in the driveway with a snow blower, sending fresh wet snow in an arc onto what had probably been the lawn.

"There," she said, pointing.

"Can't," Delbert said. "No kids. Not this year, and probably not next."

"I don't care about the roof," she said. "I want to talk to the guy with the snow blower."

"You know that's not allowed," Delbert said.

"And you know if you were right, we couldn't get hotel rooms with the Greater World money that we're earning. I want to land on his lawn."

"He doesn't have a lawn," Delbert said. "That's a pile of snow. And if we land anywhere near the removal equipment, snow will land on us and make us visible."

"So land on the other side," she said, not hiding her exasperation.

"Why is this so important to you?" he asked.

"It just is," she said. And she realized that was her answer. She couldn't leave their parting like it had been. She needed to talk with the handsome man one more time.

Delbert sighed and ran his hand on that countertop. The sleigh veered slightly to the left, making Julka lose her vision of the street and the snow blower. Then the sleigh settled out and hovered its way down, using its mechanical rudders.

The sleigh landed near that nifty staircase. Julka got out of the sleigh on the far side and sank into the snow up to her knees. She cursed (hoped Delbert didn't hear her since cursing outside the sleigh was a reportable offense), and used her rooftop magic to skim along the top of the snow to a side street. Then she brushed herself off as best she could, and walked down the icy street as if she had come from the Burger King.

She wasn't quite sure how to play this. "Yoo-hoo!" seemed too casual. "Hi!" probably impossible to hear over that blower. Walking up behind the handsome man and tapping him on the shoulder would probably scare him to death.

So she waited at the edge of the cleared-off area, and waited until he shut down the blower midway through the job, probably to take a short rest.

"Um," she said, wishing she had planned this better. "Excuse me?"

He still jumped like she had screamed at him. He

turned around fast, nearly lost his balance on the ice, and had to use the handles of the snow blower to catch himself.

"Um," he said. "Hi."

He sounded confused. Indeed, he was looking at her as if he wasn't sure if she was real.

She smiled at him and walked (carefully) up the slick driveway. "I just...you're a banker right?"

He let out a small sigh, and then shook his head. "No, I'm not a banker. I'm not anything really. I'm retired."

Judging from his tone of voice, she had asked the wrong thing. But she had committed herself to this, and she wasn't going to back off.

"Retired?" she asked. "I thought only really old people retired."

He smiled. The smile was small, reluctant, as if he didn't smile all that often. "It's a nice way of saying I quit."

So she had said something wrong again. Maybe reading and studying customs wasn't quite the same as understanding them.

"Oh," she said. "I thought in New England that retiring was mandatory at a certain age."

He frowned, then barked out a laugh. "In New England?"

"That's where we are, right?"

"Yes, but—where are you from?"

She couldn't answer that. She had to give the company's stock answer, which she felt wasn't complete enough. "Up north," she said.

"Canada?" he asked. "I thought Canadians knew about the United States. After all, we're kinda hard to miss."

"Yes," she said, "I mean, no. I mean, you *are* hard to miss."

She couldn't keep going in this direction. She was really screwing up. She understood the difference between the United States and New England, she thought, but apparently not well enough.

"I just came to talk to you after lunch—those people were so strange. They said you did something wrong, but they didn't know what."

"They just need someone to blame," he said. Then he rubbed a gloved hand over his face. "That came out wrong. It came out like I'm accusing them. I'm not. It's just—"

"You retired," she said, still not entirely understanding what that meant.

"Yes," he said.

"And you've been spending the last few—months? Years? Being nice to them."

"No," he said sadly. "I've just been trying to fit in, and that won't work."

Then he shrugged, and said, "But you didn't come here to talk about that, did you?"

"I..." her voice trailed off. She didn't have a plausible

lie. She had never been good at lying, even when she was supposed to for Santa or the kids.

So she pulled off her mitten and stuck out her hand. "I'm Julka."

"Marshall." He took her hand, but didn't shake it.

"Hi," she said, and blushed.

"Hi," he said, and shifted just a little. He hadn't let go of her hand yet.

She liked the way his hand felt, bigger and warmer than hers, enveloping hers altogether. Her eyes met his, and something shivered through her. Something better than nice.

He seemed to feel it too, because his eyes brightened. "I'd ask you to dinner," he said, "but after that lunch—"

"I know," she said. "I made a pig of myself."

"No, really," he said. "It's not that. How about coffee? It's really cold and we could have some coffee. Although I think most places aren't open. Half the town has lost power."

"Do you have power?" she asked. Besides power over her. Because he still held her hand and she didn't mind. She always minded when a man held her hand too long. And some of the elves were just plain gropey, which she didn't like at all.

"Um." Marshall glanced over his shoulder at the house. It looked way high up from here, with its odd mixture of Tudor and Colonial—and its seemingly perfect roof. "I do have power. I can make us coffee."

Her eyebrows went up. "This is your house?"

He nodded. "I thought you knew that."

She shook her head. *No kids,* Delbert had said. *Not this year, and probably not next.*

"So you're not married?" she blurted.

"No," Marshall said. That grip on her hand remained loose. The question didn't seem to bother him. "No girl-friends either. Not for the last year or so."

She wanted to say *How lonely,* but then she hadn't had a special fella for years now and she wasn't lonely. (Was she?) She had grown up with most of the guys at the North Pole, and they held no mystery for her.

She wanted mystery. She wanted difference. That was why she wanted to travel.

"I should say I'm sorry to hear that," she said, "but I'm not."

Then she smiled. She usually wasn't that forward. In fact, she couldn't ever remember being that forward, especially with a guy she knew nothing about.

"I can make you coffee inside," he said, "Or bring it out if you think that's too bold."

"It's not too bold," she said.

"It'll take maybe ten minutes to finish the driveway. If you don't mind."

"I don't mind," she said.

He smiled at her, then slowly let go of her hand. She felt the loss, not just of his warmth, but of him. She stepped back out of the way. She wished she had the skills some of the elves did. Snow removal with the snap of a finger. But her own magic was odd: seeing solutions when other people didn't even know there were problems. And the added magic she had gotten for the rooftops job hadn't helped at all.

He turned his back on her and started up the snow blower. As he went forward, someone grabbed her arm. She eeped. She didn't see anything. But she smelled peppermint and stale elf sweat.

Delbert.

"Hey," he said. "What is all this? You're not supposed to fraternize."

She could barely hear him over the snow blower, and she couldn't see him at all. He had on his invisibility shield, the same kind of shield that Santa used when a kid stumbled on him in the middle of the night. Only S-Elves could use an invisibility shield, but she'd sure like to try, if nothing else than to get rid of Delbert.

"Leave me alone," she said in the direction of the hand gripping her arm. She could see a Delbert-sized opening snow drift created by the blower. He had apparently barreled through. He had probably even left tracks all the way back to the invisible sleigh. Delbert really was not the brightest elf in the workshop.

"No," he said, tugging on her arm. "We're going to get in trouble."

And he couldn't afford any more trouble.

"If something goes wrong, I'll tell the truth," she said. "This is all my idea."

Behind her, the blower sounded louder. It was moving in a different direction. For some reason, that made her nervous. She started to turn—

When an arc of cold snow coated her. Her and Delbert.

Eight

MARSHALL WAS MOVING too fast. He hadn't been thinking. (Well, he had been thinking. Of Julka, not of anything else. Julka and coffee and the fact that she had found him, all on her own, and that she seemed nervous and she let him hold her hand and jeez, he felt like he was thirteen, only he hadn't felt this way when he was thirteen because he hadn't been able to get up enough nerve to talk to a girl, let alone touch her, or do anything until he was much, much older. College, really, and then only because he had met girls who were also interested in math and didn't mind awkwardness—and there he was, not thinking again.)

Anyway, he hadn't been thinking about blowing snow or the powerful machine vibrating under his hands.

He had been hurrying so he could get to that coffee, and hurrying never really did anyone any good. He kept going in this kinda fugue state until he heard the blower go crunch, and then make a growly noise that wasn't normal.

That caught his attention. He had probably hit some kind of decorative rock—which he really had to remove come spring. He backed the blower up, turned it sideways to get it out of the awkward position it was in, and then turned again—and walloped poor Julka with a mound of snow.

His face flushed so hot he could have powered the entire block. He shut off the blower so he could apologize (even though she did look cute, standing there in her red not-elf costume, with snow frosting her hair, eyelashes, and cheekbones) and that was when he realized that there was something else beside her.

Somehow the snow had formed a weird kinda snow man next to her. Only it looked vaguely like an unfinished Santa. Marshall had never seen the snow do anything like that, and he figured it was probably like the ways that clouds formed animal shapes—at least, he thought that until the Santa shape moved and cursed in definitively not Santa-like language.

"Hey!" the Santa shape said in a burly male voice. "We're standing here."

Its (his?) violent movement made half of the snow fall (off? Was there something to fall off of?), leaving a partial

Santa shape that reminded Marshall of nothing more than a half-eaten unfrosted Santa sugar cookie.

"Shh, Delbert," Julka said, not moving her lips. But she wasn't as quiet as she clearly thought she was, because Marshall heard her.

"There really is someone there?" he asked.

"No!" she and the male voice said in unison. Then Julka turned her head and glared at the half-Santa shape.

Marshall looked at him (it?) too, and realized that just past it was a roundish opening in the snow drift, and footprints in the snow that came from the yard somewhere.

This time, Marshall couldn't blame it on tiredness or on not having food or on his imagination. This time, he knew he was seeing something odd, and he knew it for two reasons:

One, other people in the Burger King had seen Julka. (And besides, he'd been struggling with ketchup-flavored burps ever since he left, so he had clearly been to Burger King.)

And two, if they had seen Julka, and she had come here (and she had, he knew it, because he could still conjure the sensation of her hand in his), then she was talking to the half-Santa shape, and that meant she saw it too.

In fact, that meant that she knew what it was.

"Someone want to tell me what's going on here?" Marshall asked.

"No," the male voice said.

"*Delbert!*" Julka clearly reprimanded the voice, but Marshall couldn't tell what for. For talking? For standing there? For being rude?

"Just…just…just fix it," she was saying as if that thought broke her heart.

"I can't," the voice (Delbert?) said. "I had most of my S-Elf privileges removed."

Julka rolled her eyes. "Okay, then," she said, grabbing the air in front of her and pulling.

As she did, the air waved, like a tablecloth in the breeze. Marshall wasn't sure what caused that effect. He wasn't sure he wanted to know. But his mind didn't linger on it long, because as she tugged, a round man appeared.

He had a white beard and white hair, and he was wearing sweats that clearly needed washing, and a too-small T-shirt that said, *Lobstermen do it with nets*. He looked like Santa but not really.

"You're not supposed to see me," this Delbert guy said to Marshall.

"Well, I think the reindeer missed that sleigh," Julka said, rolling her eyes.

She clearly wasn't making the comment to Marshall, who was still having a bit of trouble comprehending all of this.

"It's not my fault, really," Delbert said. "I'm supposed to have the power to make you not remember seeing me, but they took my privileges away from me, and now I can't do that. I mean, how can you blame me?"

"I can blame you," Julka said softly.

Marshall wanted to ask who "they" were, and what the "privileges" were, but he wasn't sure he would like the answer. The last time he heard the words "they" and "privileges" in an incoherent context, "they" referred to the mental health hospital staff and "privileges" meant walking the hospital grounds.

Which he didn't want to think about. Because if Delbert was off the hospital grounds, did that mean Julka was too? And how come Delbert had looked invisible? No one could become invisible. Marshall firmly believed that. If he didn't, he would need to be led along a sidewalk on the grounds, heading toward the hospital proper.

"So," Delbert was saying to Marshall, "can you just like pretend that you didn't see me? Because if an unauthorized someone ever sees me again, then I'm going to be sent home and never be allowed out again."

There it was. Hospital grounds, couched in the vague terms. Marshall closed his eyes and sighed. No wonder people emphasized the power of "nice" where Julka lived. "Nice" meant that folks with mental health issues had to learn how to get along.

It explained why she had looked so happy when she had come into Burger King. Freedom did that for folks.

It also explained why she was here. She had nowhere else to go, except back.

And somehow, he was going to have to be the one to get her there. How on Earth was he supposed to find out where she had come from without tipping his hand? The only clue she had given him was that she was from up north, but he wasn't even sure he could trust that. Did folks with mental health issues have a good sense of direction?

He had no idea.

He held up his hands as if he was being robbed. Maybe he was. Robbed of his delusions.

"I'll make sure no one knows I saw you," Marshall said to Delbert. "I promise."

"You don't have to promise him anything," Julka said. "He screwed up. He shouldn't have gotten out of the sleigh."

Then she clapped both hands over her mouth as Delbert slapped her arm.

"I didn't say that," he said. "I didn't. If they blame me for that, I'm going to give you up. I mean it, along with all that weird behavior. And *fraternizing*. You shouldn't fraternize. I told you nothing good would come of it."

Fraternize. Apparently he meant with Marshall. Apparently, these two weren't even allowed to talk to people.

Marshall let out a small sigh. A perfect capper to a perfectly bad week. He leaned back, shut off the snow blower, and tucked the key in his pocket. Then he almost put his hands up again. That robbing metaphor stuck with him, probably because he felt like he'd been robbed.

"Look, you guys are clearly far from home, and in a strange place and I'm sure that's not comfortable...."

Lord, he was babbling. Julka was staring at Marshall with such disappointment that he felt worse than he had a moment ago. He stopped talking altogether.

He had encountered yet another situation that he didn't know how to handle. He had no idea how many more of them he could take.

J ULKA'S BREATH CAUGHT. Marshall thought she was crazy. She had been warned about this reaction in all of her Greater World classes. If she talked too much about the North Pole or exhibited too much magical behavior, the people of the Greater World would dismiss her as a crazy person.

But she didn't want Marshall to think her crazy. She had liked the way he looked at her before, the interest in his eyes, the way that he smiled at her, the touch of his hand on hers. She had liked that a lot. More than a lot, actually. She had been looking forward to coffee and conversation, and stretching those 35 houses into five days worth of work, and getting to know Marshall and maybe putting in a request to meet the folks who ran the New England advance team—the entire team, not just the

Entry Access Quality Control section. Maybe she could be assigned here permanently. She liked the snow, after all.

She hadn't realized all of those dreams had been in her mind just since lunch until Marshall looked at her like she wasn't right in the head. If she could righteously punch Delbert right now, she would. But he had just been trying to save her from herself.

And failing.

But he was correct: it was her fault. She had wanted a bunch of things that were forbidden to her. And she was going to get into trouble for it.

Then she frowned.

She was going to get into trouble for it. Anyway. That's the word she was missing. She was going to get in trouble *anyway,* so why not go for broke?

It was better than finding an S-Elf who would make Marshall forget he even met her. She had momentarily been willing to follow that rule, and the pain in her chest —in her heart—had been severe.

She liked this man. She more than liked this man. This man felt—she didn't even have the word. More appropriate? Better? Right? He felt right for her.

So she was going to go for broke. And if they decided to punish her at the North Pole, so be it. Nothing could feel worse than that moment when she had asked Delbert to make Marshall forget him. Her. Them.

Make Marshall forget them.

She shoved the invisibility shield at Delbert, and hit

him with it in the stomach. She liked to think that was an accident, but it probably wasn't.

He caught it and his hands immediately disappeared. Hers didn't when she held the dang thing, but Delbert's did. Of course, someone who didn't even believe in magic probably wouldn't notice the difference.

She extended her hand to Marshall. "Come with me."

He looked at her cautiously, that what's-she-going-to-do-now look in his eye, the one that people got when she misbehaved. He hadn't used that on her before.

She had to change the look by no longer earning it.

"Please," she said.

He glanced at Delbert, blinked, and frowned. Marshall had clearly seen the missing hands. In fact, Delbert was holding the shield in front of his legs, so from the waist down, a circle of him had disappeared, leaving only the outside of his thighs, his ankles and his shoes visible.

No one could miss that. She wasn't sure how anyone could justify it to themselves, but no one could miss it.

She extended her hand just a little farther. Marshall eyed it like it might bite him, when before he had clearly enjoyed touching her.

She held her breath.

He stepped forward and took her hand firmly in his own. "All right," he said. "Where do you want to go?"

Ten

HE DIDN'T KNOW what he expected—maybe that she would lead him to his truck or to the vehicle she had stolen (because if she had escaped from an institution, she couldn't have one of her own, right?). The one thing he did know was this: He hadn't expected her to lead him through the hole in the snow.

She dragged him around Delbert, and she walked into the hole. Marshall followed.

The first thing that he noticed was that the hole was a Delbert-sized hole, and that the footprints—heading toward his driveway—were Delbert-sized footprints. But they were the only pair of prints. Marshall saw no sign of Julka's dainty prints, the ones she was now leaving on the way to—what? He couldn't tell. But he did see some flat deep marks in the snow, marks that looked like they were made by giant skis.

He felt a shiver run down his back that had nothing to do with the cold. Was someone playing a prank on him? Was this a trick to get the terrible investment banker out of the neighborhood? And if so, why do it now? Why not wait until Christmas?

He was feeling paranoid. Heck, no. He *was* paranoid. But he had to admit, if only to himself, that this afternoon —ever since he had seen Julka in Burger King (if not before) was extremely strange.

Still, it would be impossible to do such a thing in this storm, on the eve of Halloween.

He didn't say anything. He let her pull him to the marks in the snow. Of course, he did. And he felt really sad. Because he had liked her more than he had liked any woman he ever met, more than he had liked *anyone* he had ever met. He had found her intriguing and beautiful in her non-elfish way, and just odd enough to make her interesting to him.

And he had sacrificed that for her, so she could have a good trip here, thinking the memory would be enough for him. Then she had shown up here at his house, and he actually had hope for something more, something that would be—he didn't know, more than coffee, surely, more than a simple afternoon talking.

He only knew that he could have gazed in her eyes forever.

He reached her side only a second later. He wondered where the joke would go now.

Then she reached up and mimed opening a door.

Eleven

THE SMELL OF peppermint and spoiled veal wafted out of the sleigh, so strong that it made Julka choke. She hadn't realized just how filthy the interior of the sleigh had gotten.

But, she was going to get in trouble *anyway*, so she was in all the way. She was taking this risk.

Even if no one else wanted her to.

Marshall no longer looked at her like she was crazy. Now he looked at her with that sadness he'd had at the Burger King. The sadness he'd had when they talked about his life. And that made her feel even worse.

"Come with me," she said one more time, and climbed the flight of invisible steps into the sleigh.

HE STILL HELD her hand. His hand rose up as she climbed a set of steps he couldn't see.

He wasn't sure why he couldn't see them; he just knew that he couldn't. Usually he could see clear plastic or whatever it was that made the steps impossible to see against that backdrop of new fallen snow. But his eyes were really off this afternoon.

He couldn't see a thing.

Half of Julka seemed to disappear into the air. But he was holding her hand, so he knew this wasn't some optical illusion.

He felt around with the toe of his boot until he found the invisible stair, then he put the bottom of his boot on it and slid his foot forward. The toe hit the next stair, but it still looked to him like he was standing on nothing.

The illusion made him oddly uncomfortable.

The smell of peppermint mixed with rotting garbage made his stomach turn. When he reached the top of the third step, he could see Julka, standing inside a—what? He didn't have the word for it. The interior of a small RV? If it was an RV, it was a 1950s Christmas-themed RV crossed with a 1950s version of a spacecraft or an airplane cockpit.

He felt dizzy, and he realized he was holding his breath.

It was that stench.

Then he leaned back out of the door, and peered at the exterior.

There was no exterior. Only a blank spot where there should've been a view of the hedgerow between his property and the neighbor's, and the curve in the road, and from this vantage, the tip of another neighbor's house.

"Come on," she said for the third time.

Third time's the charm, his mom always used to say. He wondered what she would think now. His mom hadn't had a lot of imagination. She didn't even understand imaginary numbers, which made his mathematics brain hurt. A mathematician *needed* imagination, and his mom (face it, his parents) had none.

Although they had been proud of him. Investment banker, venture capitalist. They hadn't lived to see the collapse, didn't know about his loss of reputation, had no idea how lonely he would become.

They had always imagined him with a family—his father had said as much before the cancer took him—and that was their only disappointment. They had passed on before seeing grandchildren.

Or seeing their son lapse into complete insanity.

He stepped inside.

And immediately hit his head on the top of the door. The pain sent a shiver through him. He grabbed his forehead with his free hand. The door's opening had to be really low for him to hit his head because he was not quite six feet tall. And everything in America was built to accommodate a six-foot tall man.

But Julka had an accent, and she had made it clear she wasn't from here.

She was from up north. And she had looked a bit confused when he mentioned Canada, so maybe it wasn't that up north, but a different up north.

And she was wearing a red Santa/elf costume.

His stomach twisted—and not from the smell. Oddly enough, he was getting used to that. His stomach twisted because he was getting suspicious.

He didn't like what he was thinking.

He hadn't thought about impossible things since he got his doctorate, when he realized that impossible imaginings and mathematical theories weren't practical enough to help him survive in the real world. He'd moved to statistical analysis and mathematical systems and economics, and had made a fortune, but had screwed up his life.

So, for a moment anyway, he was going to settle on one impossible thing: A pretty non-elf woman in a Christmas costume on the day before Halloween, standing inside an invisible RV decorated like Santa's 1950 Christmas nightmare.

Marshall stood up slowly so that he didn't hit his head on the rounded ceiling. It looked like the ceiling in a camper, not the ceiling in an RV. Modern RVs, they looked like small houses. There was nothing house-like about this place. It was crammed with stuff, including some filthy t-shirts that had crude sayings on them, often with drawings. They, like everything else he'd seen so far, were Delbert-sized.

In one corner, there was a shelf covered with dainty things. That had to belong to Julka.

Marshall moved in a slow circle, taking it all in. Could this be an hallucination? Those usually didn't come with touch and stink. An illusion? Again, those were usually aimed at the eye, not the other senses. And he was wrong about the stink. It didn't just use up one sense. It imposed on two. He could taste that rot. Peppermint would never be a happy fragrance for him again.

Julka just watched him, looking a little tense.

"Okay," he said after a moment. "My first response is that you gotta explain this."

She opened her mouth, but he held up his hand so that she couldn't speak.

"My second response is that you don't dare explain

this." His heart was pounding. "Because if you explain it, then I'm going to have to think about it, and if I think about it, then I'm going to have accept some things that I'm not willing to accept—or, at least, something that I haven't accepted for oh, twenty-some years."

Her mouth closed, and she tilted her head, looking both bemused and worried.

"Not," he said, "that I'm close-minded or anything. It's just that I'm—oh, God—not willing to change cherished beliefs, which makes me close-minded, I guess, or maybe just adult, because if I take this at face value, then that means Santa is real, and if Santa is real, then all of those science courses I took, all of those courses that I *believed* in, they would be wrong."

Julka raised a finger, as if she were going to say something. And he really should let her talk, but he couldn't stop babbling, because if he stopped, then she would tell him what he was seeing, and that would be a bad thing.

A very bad thing.

"And if the science courses are wrong, well, that's less serious than the math courses being wrong, because I *believe* in math, and it is a mathematical impossibility for one man to circle the globe in 24 hours *and* drop off the right toys at the right house without anyone seeing him. Just on the time factor alone. There aren't enough minutes in the day. There just aren't. And that's for the flying and the landing. That's not really counting the time it would take to squeeze down a chimney."

Then his breath caught. He first saw her on *rooftops.* Looking at chimneys. He'd seen her *kick* a chimney.

But he couldn't think about that right now. So he kept talking. Because if he let her talk, then she might say something sensible. (How could there be anything sensible about this?) And he would have to listen, and if he listened, then—

"Maybe I can deal with the loss of science," he said, "but the loss of math—well, that's like the final straw. Because I devoted my life to math. Until this moment, I *understood* math. I have always understood math. That's why I retired when I couldn't convince the guys in my office that the way they were floating on one of those proverbial mathematical bubbles and those things didn't last, but if this is all true, well then, this bubble has lasted, and everything, *everything,* I know is wrong, and I really really really can't face that. Not right now."

Julka's shoulders drooped. He had disappointed her. Worse, he had hurt her somehow. He wasn't sure how, but he had.

"It's not about math," she started.

"Of course it's about math." He sounded even more panicked than he felt. He sounded terrified and wobbly and slightly off-the-beam. Maybe more than slightly off-the-beam. "Don't you understand? That's how I knew Santa wasn't real. I did the damn math."

"I understand math," Julka said, moving her hands just a little in a "calm down" gesture. Now she was treating him as if he was the one who was crazy, and maybe he was. This entire idea had left him so unsettled that off-the-beam was really the wrong way to describe it. Off his nut might've been better.

"Really," she said, taking a step toward him. "I *love* math. It was one of my best subjects in school, and I use it all the time, because I love organizing."

He almost said with a mathematician's sneer, *That's not math. That's arithmetic.* But he needed to shut up now. He needed to stop talking and let her say something.

"Math is a phenomenal thing," Julka was saying. "You can represent it with sticks on the simplest level—you know, one-plus-one-equals-two kinda thing. Then math starts getting really complex, and you have to *imagine* it and sometimes you have to trust it, and there are pockets of it and corners of it that no one understands at all."

His breath caught. She did know math. Not arithmetic. *Math.*

"I have a hunch, if you come back home with me, you'll find some people who can explain the math and the science to you. It's elegant." She glanced at what looked like several old-fashioned TV sets, but through one of them, he could see the neighborhood. He could see his driveway.

Delbert was missing. Was that important?

"You're telling me that it's not magic. It's science." Marshall couldn't quite keep the sarcasm from his voice.

"I seem to recall reading a book when I was a kid that

said that all science looks like magic to those who don't understand it," Julka said.

She was quoting Arthur C. Clarke. A science-fiction writer. One of Marshall's favorite writers when he was a kid. How long had it been since he had read something for fun?

How long had it been since he had fun?

Then he wondered if he was supposed to be wondering that. Was there something in this sleigh/RV/invisible thing that made him think thoughts he didn't want? That magicked him?

He sank into a nearby chair. It was large and it smelled of peppermint. He popped out of it quickly.

"So you're saying it's all science," Marshall repeated.

"I'm saying I don't know." Julka came closer to him. "But what if it is magic and not science? What's wrong with that?"

"It's not possible—"

"Most things aren't possible," she said. "*Bumblebees* aren't possible, yet they exist. Soul mates aren't possible, yet people always say they found theirs."

She bit her bottom lip as if she had said something she hadn't planned on saying.

Soul mates. His parents said they were each other's soul mates and believed it too. He had done the math on that as well, and figured with billions of people on Earth that the odds of finding the one person who suited you were—well, billions to one. So he figured (but he never said to his parents) that everyone had a bunch of soul mates, and it was all chemical, and none of that explained the look in Julka's eyes.

The anticipation, with a bit of fear. The fact that her pupils were slightly dilated which, he had learned in some long-ago biology class, was a sign of attraction.

And it didn't explain how it bothered him to hurt her or to upset her or how he just wanted to take her hands in his and pull her forward and kiss her silly.

He'd never done anything that bold in his entire life.

"Why did you bring me here?" he asked softly.

She shrugged and looked away. "I was going to get in trouble anyway."

"For what?"

She bowed her head. "Fraternizing."

"With me?"

"With anyone who wasn't, you know, someone I had to talk to, like one of the employees at Burger King."

Marshall frowned. "You'd get in trouble for talking to me. Why?"

"We have illusions to keep up," she said, head still down, voice almost a whisper. "The entire world thinks Santa does this alone."

No, Marshall wanted to say, *we're taught that he has elves.* And then Marshall realized that they were taught about the elves in the *workshop,* not elves outside of the workshop. Not elves on the rooftops of Connecticut.

"You were scouting out chimneys," he said, less as a question and more as a realization.

"No, not exactly," she said. "I'm tasked with looking for the best entry locations on the proper houses."

Corporate speak. She was actually using corporate speak.

"How big is this organization?" Marshall asked.

She shrugged. "I don't know. Are you asking money or personnel?"

"Both, I guess," he said, suddenly unable to visualize paying for everything he knew about the fictional Santa.

"I'm not privy to the money side," she said, "but it's huge. And we have millions of employees worldwide, not all of them human."

Not all of them human. He tried not to let his brain turn to mush at that statement. "You mean reindeer, and stuff."

"Elves," she said. "They're not human. Delbert's not human."

"He's an elf?" Marshall asked.

"He's an S-Elf," Julka said. "From Santa's line. Those are the most important elves of all."

"Wow," Marshall said, believing it, then wondering if he should believe it, and then wondering if the sleigh (this was a sleigh, right?) made him believe it, and then wondering if he should believe that the sleigh made him believe.

So he gave up wondering at all.

"But you're human," he said, and it was more of a hope than a question.

She nodded. "A lot of families got hired real early on to humanize the whole procedure and most of them stayed. My family goes back twenty-five generations at the North Pole."

He did the arithmetic in his head: Twenty-five generations, at roughly twenty years per generation, was—

"Five hundred years?" he blurted.

"Give or take," she said.

"So you grew up at the North Pole?" he asked. "I thought it's desolate there."

"It's not the North Pole that you can travel to," she said. "It's like this sleigh. We have a different North Pole that you can access—or rather, I can access—through your North Pole."

His North Pole. He'd never seen the North Pole. Either one, actually.

"And you now work as what—Santa's advance team?" he asked.

"Kinda," she said. "I'm probably going to get fired for this."

"For bringing me here," he said.

She nodded miserably.

"What happens when you get fired?" he asked.

She shrugged a shoulder. "I'll probably have to go back to training school, and they'll find me a job at the

Pole. I really, really, really wanted to spend my time in the Greater World."

"Which is—?"

"Your world," she said. "I wanted to man one of the advance headquarters, you know, have a permanent place here."

"And you risked all that to talk to me?" he asked. "Why?"

"I don't know." She raised her head. "You just seemed important somehow."

"Important to...?"

"Me," she said miserably. "Important to me."

No one had thought him important for years. Not since his parents died. And then, he wasn't their main priority. They were each other's main priority. He was second on their list and had been from the beginning. He had known that almost as soon as he started breathing.

"Why would I be important to you?" he asked. "We just met."

"I know," she said. "It's stupid, isn't it?"

He took her hands. She was trembling.

"No," he said. "No. It's not stupid."

He wanted to say it was an honor, but that actually sounded like he was dismissing it. And if he said *You're important to me too,* it would sound like he was just trying to make her feel better, and he wasn't.

"I'm standing here," he said, "and you're making me rethink everything I've ever known, and honestly, I'm not fleeing, which is what I usually do when I'm challenged. I turn away. And I don't want to."

Her gaze met his. Her eyes were big and blue and incredibly beautiful. "Why?"

"Because," he whispered, "I found another place where the math doesn't work."

"What—?" she asked.

"Soul mates," he said. "It's mathematically ridiculous."

She nodded, and tried to pull her hands from his.

"But I've never felt anything like this before," he said. "So right, so perfect, as if we were made for each other."

Her eyes filled with tears, but they didn't fall. He leaned forward and kissed the corner of one eye, tasting salt, tasting her. Then he showered kisses down the side of her face until she tilted her head toward him.

Their mouths met, and tentatively, hesitantly, they kissed. Then the kiss got deeper, and he finally understood what his parents talked about: that rightness, that sense he had found his other half, that sense of perfection, of—

"Oh, no," said a male voice. Delbert's voice. "Now I really will have to report this."

<h1 style="text-align:center">Thirteen</h1>

THE SLEIGH ROCKED as Delbert climbed inside. He put both hands on the side of the door as if he was blocking someone's escape, but Julka didn't know whose.

It certainly wouldn't be her. She didn't want to move. She hadn't wanted to break the kiss, but Marshall had done so, looking startled—again.

She almost brought her fingers to her mouth in amazement. She had never been kissed like that. She had never felt anything like that before. Never.

And she wanted to feel it again.

"Report?" Marshall asked, sounding a bit unsettled. "To whom?"

"You'd think it'd be to the big guy," Delbert said, "but he doesn't handle small personnel matters. Still, this is one of those things. I don't like reporting anyone for fraternization, Julka, especially since I know how it can go, but I'm on double-secret forever probation, and if I don't and they find out, I'll never be able to leave the North Pole again. I'm sorry."

He sounded sorry. She had never seen him look so upset, actually. He reached over to that flat countertop area and touched a red button she'd never noticed before.

And then he vanished.

"What?" Marshall said. "What was that? Is he still here?"

"No," Julka said. She felt heavy suddenly. Her legs wouldn't support her, and she had to grope for one of the chairs before she sat down. She had known it was a risk bringing Marshall here, but somehow she hadn't thought Delbert would report her. Maybe he wouldn't have without the kiss. Or maybe he was just giving her a chance to come to her senses.

Which she hadn't.

She still didn't regret this, no matter what the consequences.

"Where did he go?" Marshall asked.

"Headquarters," she said miserably. "They're going to bring the goon squad here, and they'll clean up after me."

"How will they do that?" Marshall asked.

She didn't want to tell him, although it really didn't matter if she told him. None of this would matter to him in...oh, five minutes or so.

But she didn't want to lie to him, not even now, not when she could leap back into his arms and kiss him senseless until the goon squad got here.

"They'll wipe your memory," she said. "Delbert should have done it, but they've limited his powers."

She had asked Delbert to do it, but that was before the kiss. It had broken her heart then. It would destroy her now.

Oddly, it felt like she had known this man her entire life—or maybe, it felt like she *would* know this man her entire life. Better than anyone else.

But that was going away too.

Her hands were shaking.

"They'll make me forget?" Marshall asked. "They can do that? With magic?"

"I don't know how they do it," she said tiredly. "I just know that they do. S-Elves can. Santa can. To protect the myth, you know. It's all about protecting the myth."

"From what?" Marshall asked.

She shook her head. "We're supposed to control the message."

"And the message is that pretty women can't kiss men they're interested in?"

"No," she said. "We can't fraternize. You're not part of the community. You can't know about us, and I told."

She worse than told. She showed him everything that she could in the short time allowed. *He'd been inside the sleigh*. No one got inside the sleigh. No one except people with clearance.

She hadn't even had clearance until a few months ago.

"I can't forget this," he said. "This is life-changing."

"I know," she said. And she did. That was why the secrets never got out. They made sensible men kiss women like her. They made sensible men deny their belief in science for a grasp at the hope of Christmas magic. They made—

"No," Marshall said. "You don't know. You think I'm talking about Santa. I'm talking about you."

She froze, just for a moment. What had he said? Her? Really? He found her life-changing like she had found him life-changing?

"I can't forget you," he said. "You're the best thing that has ever happened to me, and I mean ever. Even if I never see you again, I can't forget you."

"They won't let that happen," she said, resisting the urge to look at her watch. She wanted to know how much time was left before the goon squad arrived, but she didn't want to know at the same time. "You can't remember me. Only insiders know this stuff. I should've thought it through."

"Insiders," he said, kneeling in front of her and taking her shoulders in his hands. His hands were warm, strong. She liked his hands. "You mean people who work at the North Pole—your North Pole."

"Yes," she said.

He kissed her. "Julka, you're brilliant."

He let go of her and bounded over to that countertop where the red button still glowed. He slapped his hand on the button and nothing happened. Then he kept pounding.

"I don't know how to make you hear me," he shouted at the screens, "but give me a job. Surely you have use for a mathematician who understands business and statistics and real money management. I can streamline your business. I can make it more efficient. I know how to save money without changing personnel or making you lose any of your goodwill. I can—"

His voice cut out first. And then he shimmered. And finally, he disappeared.

Julka ran to the countertop. The button was gone. Delbert was gone. *Marshall* was gone.

Something had happened, and she didn't entirely understand it.

Correction: she didn't understand it at all.

Fourteen

ONE MINUTE HE was standing in that weird 1950s RV sleigh, the next he was inside a badly decorated 1950s office, complete with single-pane windows frosting up against the cold outside, a humidifier trying to keep moisture in the dry air, a blond desk and matching chair, and a square console television set in the corner, its bulging screen showing the inside of that 1950s RV sleigh, with Julka frantically pressing the countertop he had just been touching.

The room smelled of coffee and cookies. The walls were covered in flocked candy cane wallpaper, and someone had wrapped a green ribbon around the back of the couch. A poinsettia sat on the blond wood end table, and the happy faces of cartoon carolers decorated the window above the door.

The transition made Marshall feel dizzy, but he felt weirdly comfortable too, for the first time in years. It took only a moment for him to understand why: this was a corporate environment—a corporate environment decorated for Christmas (on the day before Halloween), but a corporate environment all the same.

He turned toward the desk. A woman of indeterminate age sat behind it. She had a beehive hairdo dyed so black that it looked like the color would smear on her fingers if she touched it. She wore a lot of make-up, also making it impossible to determine her age, including bright red lipstick that matched her bright red fingernails. A cigarette that he couldn't smell smoldered in a red and green ashtray that said, "Keep the Happy in Christmas!"

The combination of the words "happy" and "Christmas" collided in his head, and therefore, he wasn't surprised when the woman spoke to him in a working class English accent.

"So," she said, "you think you have something to offer Claus & Company."

Apparently, she wasn't at all surprised by his appearance. Apparently, she had something to do with it.

He bowed his head just a little. It had been a decade or more since he had had a job interview. There were no chairs on this side of the desk. He felt like he should have a hat in his hands—a supplicant.

"I've got more than a decade in finance," he said. "I know how to make companies more efficient—"

"We're familiar with you American efficiency types," she said. "You cut staff to the bone, get rid of markets that are underperforming, and while the business makes a profit, the customers are deeply dissatisfied. We are in the customer satisfaction business, not the profit business."

He nodded. He wasn't dressed for this. He didn't have his resume or any papers with him. All he had were his wits, which, he had to admit, were getting a bit tired on this day.

"I-I know," he said. "It's something I've decried for my entire career. I got let go from my finance job when I tried to convince the company that they were hurting the very people they were trying to help. I used statistics and math to show that a long-term view would make them more profitable down the road, and it would bring in more customers, and everyone would be happy, but that didn't—"

"Honestly, Mr. Collier, we at Claus & Company don't care about your Greater World concerns," the woman said. "What we care about is what you can bring to us."

Marshall opened his hands a little. "Normally, ma'am, I research a company before I talk to anyone involved with it. But I've been a bit blindsided here. I didn't know you existed until today—"

"You knew," she said in a chiding tone. "Everyone

knows about us. Then they 'grow up' and 'lose sight of childish things.' You were one of those, I suppose."

His cheeks flushed. "The real world—what you call the Greater World…?"

She nodded. That hair moved with her head like it weighed a ton.

"…it can be a harsh and disillusioning place." He shrugged. "I let it disillusion me."

"And still, you're here," she said, picking up that cigarette and tapping an inch of ash off the end. The cigarette got no shorter. "You can't be entirely disillusioned."

"Julka convinced me," he said, wondering if he should speak her name, wondering if he would get her in trouble. "Only a fool denies what's in front of him, and she placed it all in front of me."

"She's quite attractive, eh?" the woman asked.

They knew. They knew everything, and he was dancing around it all like a fool.

"I like her a lot," he said. "More than I've ever liked anyone. I won't lie to you, ma'am. The idea of losing the memory of this day, even if I never see her again, is more than I can bear."

"So you're just here to get the girl," the woman said.

He shook his head. "You people give others hope. Even if they don't want it, they brighten up for just one day. They smile for a moment. I've learned these last few years that those smiles are important."

The woman stared at him and tapped more ash off her cigarette.

"Yes," he said. "I'm here because of Julka, because she brought something bright and magical and wonderful into my life. I expect I won't see her again. I expect you to send me on my way. But please, don't make me forget her. Those moments—even if they're fleeting—are the most important thing in life."

The woman still stared at him. Didn't she have any emotions?

"I have been trying to make up for all I did at my previous work," he said. "I've been doing my best, but I'm flailing around. Being here would give me focus. It would make me remember that there are people behind the numbers. Even when the numbers are impossible."

The woman put the cigarette in her mouth and took a drag. He still couldn't smell the dang thing, which was a good thing; he didn't like the smell of cigarette smoke. But it was a bit freaky.

"If you came to work for us," she said, "you would get benefits. Your life would be extended by perhaps a century or more. You would be given small magic via spell that would have to be renewed annually. You would get housing and clothing and all of your needs provided for."

He swallowed. He'd been through these kinds of interviews before. He knew there was a "but" coming.

"But," she said rather loudly, "you won't be able to tell your family what you do, and when it becomes obvious that you're not aging at the same rate they are, you will have to forgo seeing them altogether. You won't be able to talk to your friends about this either. You will get two weeks annual vacation which you can take in the Greater World, but you cannot do so in the fall or over Christmas. The sacrifice is often greater than the average mortal can make."

He couldn't say anything about his friends. His friends had pretty much disowned him when he retired. The new friends that he could have had after that were mostly after his money. So he just said, "My family is gone."

"Well then." The woman stood, set down that weird cigarette, and extended her hand. "You're hired."

That surprised him too. What a surprising day. But the surprise wasn't enough to make him lose focus.

He shook the woman's hand.

"Thank you," he said, and he meant it. Who knew when he got up that morning that by the middle of the day he would be giving up everything, and realizing that by doing so, he was giving up nothing at all.

"You will go back to Julka and await your instructions," the woman said. "Congratulations. We at Claus & Company hope that our relationship with you is long and merry."

"Me, too," Marshall said. "Me too."

J ULKA KEPT HITTING the countertop.

"C'mon," she said. "I know someone can see me. What did you do with him? Take me to him. He has no idea what home is like. *Please.*"

She had no idea where he was. Had Marshall hit the red button that was still pulsing there and had it sent him where Delbert was? Or did someone actually hear him make his offer, and take him to the North Pole somehow. She had no idea how that would work for a non-elf. Even elves had to use sleigh magic. Had Marshall somehow triggered something?

"Please," she said, not quite sure any more what she was begging for. "Please."

Her hand hurt from hitting the console. She was going to have to come up with something else. They had told her about an emergency way to contact the North Pole if something happened to Delbert, but she hadn't really paid attention. Nothing ever happened to elves. Particularly elves that stank of peppermint and elf sweat.

Then she realized she was *smelling* peppermint and elf sweat. She turned around. Delbert was watching her, his head tilted, looking amused.

"At first," he said, "I thought maybe you were one of those people who fell in crap and came out looking like gold. But the longer my conversation with HR went on, the more I realized you were sent to recruit someone. And damn, if you didn't manage it. You know, you could've told me."

She didn't know what he was referring to. Crap? Conversation? Recruit? "Told you what?"

"That you weren't here to inspect chimneys. I should've figured it out. You weren't the chimney inspecting type. And you got frustrated when there were too many pipes and not enough bricks. The usual chimney worker doesn't really care." He tugged on his shirt, pulling it down over his massive belly.

"I was too here to inspect chimneys," she said. "I didn't lie to you."

His eyebrows went up. "You mean that, don't you?"

"Yes, I mean that," she said.

He bit his lower lip, then rolled his eyes and sighed. "Ah. They sent you here on a test, and left it up to me to tell you."

"What?" she asked. She had been frustrated before he showed up. Now she was ready to grab him and shove his hand against the console (repeatedly) so she could find Marshall.

"That guy," Delbert said, "you know, the one you were kissing? Which I don't think they planned on, to tell the truth."

Her cheeks flushed, but she didn't care. "What about Marshall? Is he all right?"

"He's in Human Resources right now," Delbert said, "getting interviewed for his new job. They think you did great. He was a better catch than they expected, but they had to grill him. They didn't want him to show up just because he wanted to be in your pants."

"*What?*" she asked.

Delbert shrugged. "You were the one who wanted a real job, not some workshop management position. A chance to get out into the Greater World, you said. Well, the job choices are limited, but the best ones are the recruiters, because they can go anywhere. Only I'd never met one before, had you?"

It was taking Julka a few minutes to catch up. "You're saying they tested me. As a *recruiter*?"

"Yeah," Delbert said and grinned. "Although I'm really not sure they're going to want you to kiss each recruit to get him to come to the North Pole."

"I didn't kiss him because I was recruiting him," Julka

said. "I like him. I have never kissed anyone like that before."

"Well," said a voice from beside her. "That's good to hear."

Marshall was standing there. He was wearing just a bit of glitter—the kind that rubbed off flocked candy cane wallpaper. It got on *everything*.

She threw herself in his arms. "I'm sorry, I'm sorry, I'm sorry," she said. "I didn't know."

"I gathered that," Marshall said.

"They manipulated us into recruiting you. I didn't mean it," she said.

He pulled back just a little. "You don't want me to work at the North Pole?" he asked.

She didn't, not if it meant she was working here. But that wasn't what he meant, and she knew it. "I didn't know about the recruitment or the test."

"I know," he said.

"I really *like* you," she said.

"I know that too," he said.

"I...." *want to spend the rest of my life with you. Never want to leave your side.* All of that was too forward this soon, although it didn't feel soon.

"It's okay," he said, pulling her close again. "I like you too. I more than like you. It looks like I'm changing my entire life for you."

"No," she said. "You can't. You can't base a relation-ship on that."

"Is that what you want?" he asked. "A relationship?"

Her breath caught. "Don't you?"

He smiled. A real smile without sadness. "Of course I do," he said, and then he leaned in to kiss her.

Delbert cleared his throat. "You guys realize that you're going to need me."

Could Delbert get any more annoying? "For what?" Julka asked.

"The second test. Your first planned event. Seems someone figured out that the kids here weren't going to trick or treat because of the snow, so they'll need some kind of open house, complete with candy and costumes. I'm told that you have to organize it pronto, with enough advertising that the kids can find you."

Julka turned inside Marshall's arms. "What? We don't celebrate Halloween."

"But everyone here does," Marshall said. "So they told me I needed to show how well I could plan something—and do it fast—and so I thought of this."

"And then they told me that you'd need S-Elf assistance, so I'm going to assist," Delbert said, straightening up proudly.

Julka thought it all through. It only took a moment, but she realized what had just happened. She had gotten her Christmas wish. Wishes, actually. The ones she never talked about.

The ability to stay in the Greater World if she wanted.

The chance to do a job she would love—organizing. And someone beside her. Someone who would love her and cherish her. Someone she would love and cherish.

"Delbert," she said. "We need some privacy."

"Then I suggest you leave here," Delbert said. "They can turn on the monitors any time."

Marshall slid his hand along her back and said softly, "My house is right outside."

"And besides," Delbert said loudly, as if he didn't want to hear any of that. "I have to find a great venue, and that'll take the sleigh. So get out."

They didn't have to be told twice. Julka took Marshall's hand and led him out of the sleigh. They barely made it down the steps when the sleigh took off, displacing the snow, and sending a huge greasy waft of peppermint-colored exhaust into the air.

"Is that normal?" Marshall asked, looking at the red-and-white smoke glistening around them.

"None of this is normal," Julka said.

"Oh, I don't know," Marshall said. "Men, women, kisses, soul mates. Seems normal enough to me."

He wrapped his arms around her again.

She giggled. "I thought you didn't believe in soul mates."

"I didn't believe in Santa either," he said. "Yet somehow, you managed to change my mind. In an instant. On both things."

Then he kissed her.

And kept kissing her as much as he could for the rest of their long, magical lives.

Visions of Sugar Plums

TURN THE PAGE TO FALL IN LOVE WITH
MORE OF SANTA'S FAMILY

Visions of Sugar Plums

CHAPTER ONE

THE TV FRITZED. Nissa Kealoha clasped her hands behind her, trying to remain calm. She could have predicted the fritz. Greater World technology didn't work well in the North Pole. Even Greater World technology supposedly modified for North Pole needs.

She stood just inside the door of the television room at Image Headquarters, suppressing a sigh. Pipe, cigar, and cigarette smoke floated around the room like a cloud. The entire place smelled like an ashtray.

Oh, how she missed New York's nanny state. She liked to breathe. But things were different here in at the North Pole. Older, slower to change. And she had to keep reminding herself of that.

She stepped through the veil of yellow smoke into the

room proper. Her eyes stung. She couldn't see an empty chair. The room was filled with all of the advanced Image Specialists, the ones who refused to leave the North Pole.

Theoretically these people knew how to manage Santa's image, when in reality, all they knew was how to massage the Great Man's ego. Not that he had much of one. Santa truly was a Jolly Old Elf, concerned with children and toys and happiness. He didn't care about his brand, unless something interfered with it.

And the Image Specialists seemed to believe that this latest crisis interfered with the brand.

"Nissa," said Oskar, the head Image Specialist. Oskar had held the position for at least seventy years, after many successful years in the field. "Come join us."

He patted the chair beside him, directly across from the fritzing television screen. He, at least, had given up smoking a decade ago. Which didn't help a lot, considering how many other Image Specialists were puffing on something. She counted five cigarettes, two cigars, and five pipes, and those were the ones she could see.

One of the younger Image Specialists, a woman whose name Nissa could never remember, messed with a DVD player. Another female Image Specialist whispered something about thumb drives and internet hookups.

Nissa knew neither thumb drives nor internet hookups would work. Discounting the smoke, which had to have a major impact on electronics, the technology faced a larger problem.

The technology was made in the Greater World. This particular version of the North Pole didn't exist in the Greater World. This North Pole was in its own magical sideways universe, one that sort of *looked* like the Greater World, but *wasn't* the Greater World.

And the real techs at the North Pole, the ones who could handle Greater World gadgets, worked in Tech Toys, a protected area that separated technology from the magical energy which filled the Pole.

Nothing protected the technology in Image Head-quarters. And, to make matters worse, the conference room's natural magic was considerable: the oak table had ancient spirits in it, the glass table top was made of sand from magical beaches, and the thickly upholstered chairs were spelled for comfort. The people magic was consider-able as well.

Oskar was the most powerful mage in the room. He could create an image with a thought. He'd lived in the Greater World for more than a century, and had finally come back here as a reward. Nissa didn't want a reward like that. The longer she stayed at the Pole, the antsier she got.

But she did know how Oskar had become the most powerful Image mage. He'd done it through hard work. In the 1860s, he'd been the one to convince illustrator Thomas Nast to draw Santa Claus every year, a stroke of genius superseded only by the Coca-Cola ads of the 1930s (also Oskar's idea—planted in the mind of greedy cola executives).

Nissa used to admire Oskar—okay, to be fair, she *still* admired him, but she now knew that his knowledge of the Way Things Worked In The Greater World was horribly, awfully, terribly out of date.

She didn't say that as she sat down next to him. He smiled at her absently, like an indulgent father. He was old enough to be her great-great-grandfather, although he didn't look it, with his pale blond hair and unlined face. He kept himself trim, which accented his great height, something that marked him as extremely extraordinary in a world of fat elves.

She wasn't fat either. She had to stay media-perfect—American media perfect. Ten pounds too thin (just right for the cameras), athletic and toned, expertly trimmed hair, and very white teeth, "blazingly white," one of the Image execs at the far end of the table had said one afternoon. Not that he should talk; his teeth were brown from centuries of pipe tobacco and a fondness for hot cocoa before bed every night.

Most everyone in the room was white and male, except for the two fiddling with the technology and Nissa herself. Nissa didn't look like anyone else. She had black hair (most didn't), cocoa-colored skin (most didn't), black eyes (most didn't), and a smile that her mother called pure Hawaiian (thanks to her father, may he rest in peace).

Nissa fit into New York, where no one noticed how

different she was. Nissa, who had a beloved apartment on the Upper West Side in New York, New York, the city so nice they named it twice. She missed both the city and the apartment more than she wanted to admit.

"How's your mom?" Oskar asked, ever so polite.

"Better," Nissa said. Her mother had severe diabetes, a heart condition, and a reluctance to get medical treatment. Nissa wanted to take her mother to the Greater World for care, but her mother wouldn't hear of it, even though the magical doctors in the Pole had done everything they could.

As they reminded Nissa every time she visited, magic had its limits. It could extend a human life, provided the human was healthy when she got the magical life extension, but magic could not prevent death—something Nissa had learned the hard way when her father had had a massive heart attack ten years ago. He'd been dead before he hit the floor, the doctors said, and then they told her that they wouldn't revive him.

To do so here, they said, would invoke black magic—even if they used Greater World techniques. All of the magical in the various magical realms were terrified of having their magic sink into evil, but here, at the North Pole, they were downright phobic about it.

Which was why she wanted to take her mother away from here to help her get healthy. At least Greater World doctors weren't afraid that normal, life-saving techniques might make them evil. In fact, Greater World doctors believed that saving lives was not only part of their jobs, but part of the reason that they were on the side of angels.

(If only they had met some of those angels they sided with; they might reconsider.)

The television fritzed again, then popped. One of the women near the screen cursed.

"Can't you just tell me what's going on instead of trying to fix that?" Nissa asked. She didn't want to be in this room any longer than she had to.

"We wanted you to see it," Oskar said. "Weirdly, it's actually getting traction, and the Big Guy himself is concerned."

The Big Guy was Santa. But Nissa couldn't trust Oskar's statement. She didn't know if the Big Guy was concerned or not. His *handlers* might have been concerned. Usually, they didn't bother the Big Guy with anything outside of the toys, children, and humanitarian concerns of the operation. He had more than enough to do every day; he didn't need branding or image worries too.

Oskar might have been the only one truly concerned, and he might have been speaking with the royal "we." Or rather, the fantastical "we," since Santa, for all his importance, had no royal blood.

"Got it," one of the women said as an image flashed across the gigantic TV screen.

The image showed a standard talk show set. Judging from the golds and yellows, this show was American daytime, probably morning, filled with "news" and happy talk. Nissa hated happy talk, and she shouldn't. Half of what she did influenced the happy talk hosts. They were Santa's biggest media supporters in the weeks before Christmas Day.

The camera panned onto a dark-haired man wearing tweed. "...unhealthy lifestyle," he was saying. He had a rich, deep voice, an actor's voice. A singer's voice. A Voice-voice, her trainer had once called it. A gift from the gods, and magic in and of itself.

Then the image winked out. The woman in front of the television cursed and bent over the technology again.

The sound continued, even though the images did not.

"...has lots of nasty habits. The examples he sets aren't good ones. Let's not even discuss the sugar, although we should, given his girth. Let's talk about the homes where he gets a glass of eggnog alongside those cookies. Eggnog, in most places, is laced with rum. And then what does he do? He gets into his vehicle and drives to the next location. After one or two of those, he's probably tipsy. Anyone would be. But I can't imagine that he would be merely tipsy. He's spending twenty-four hours plus eating cookies and drinking rum. His capacity for alcohol..."

"*This* is what you wanted me to hear?" Nissa asked. "Some rant against Santa?"

"This is not a rant," Oskar said. "We can ignore rants. This is an amazingly well-put-together argument, perfectly pitched toward America's concern with obesity and overindulgence. The country's ripe for this kind of discussion, and we all know that where the United States goes on this holiday stuff, the world follows."

Well, that wasn't true. Large sections of the Greater World didn't celebrate Christmas at all. Large sections of the United States didn't celebrate Christmas either. Nissa's neighborhood in New York had as many Jews as Christians, and the neighborhood two blocks away was mostly Muslim. She had no idea how many people in New York City actually celebrated Christmas as a religious holiday, and how many simply ignored it, letting the seasons and the seasonal holidays wash over them like rain.

But once upon a time, Oskar had lived in a rarefied United States, one that closed its eyes to differences—or discriminated against them. Nissa wasn't sure if he left before or after 1950, but it didn't matter. He missed the Civil Rights Movement, the Women's Movement, the Gay Rights Movement, and dozens of other movements.

Plus, he still had a Eurocentric Greater Worldview, something she had tried to argue him out of, and failed.

"People have made the argument this guy's making before," Nissa said. "In 2009, *The British Medical Journal* suggested that Santa eat carrots and ride a bicycle, just so that children would understand a healthy lifestyle. I'm the one who killed that story by having everyone cover it. Every single reporter laughed at it, which was exactly what I intended."

"I know," Oskar said. "Your solution was brilliant. Which is why I'm assigning you this."

She sighed, and stifled a cough as she got a mouthful of smoke. She'd have to take a shower after she left here.

"This sounds like the same kind of thing," she said. "I'll assign it to a member of my staff when I get back."

Which she hoped would be Real Soon Now. Since everyone at the North Pole was focused on Christmas, the tension here in the holiday season was outrageous. She hated the North Pole at Christmas.

New York, on the other hand, was beautiful at this time of year.

"What this young man is arguing is not the same kind of thing," Oskar said. "This time, the argument isn't coming out of a medical journal. It's coming from Professor Ryan Palmer, a deadly combination of good looks, charm, and brilliance. He's entertaining, passionate, witty, and on a damn mission."

Oskar leaned forward and frowned at the television. The Voice-voice—Ryan Palmer, apparently—was chuckling, and saying, "...yes, I know it sounds ridiculous, but we've seen that imagery impacts belief. Smoking has gone down since cigarette advertising was banned on television in 1970, and by eliminating child-friendly icons like Joe Camel, fewer young people..."

Nissa glanced around the room to see if anyone was hearing that argument. The Image Specialists didn't even smoke less as Palmer talked about smoking declining.

They just clung to their cigarettes or puffed on their pipes, as if something like a Greater World Voice-voice couldn't screw up their bad habits.

"Can't you get the picture back?" Oskar asked one of the other women.

"Trying," the woman closest to him said.

Nissa tried to focus on the task at hand, which was, she was beginning to realize, letting Oskar know that Palmer wasn't a threat. Nissa didn't want to spend the holiday season arguing with some professor, as if she were his perfect foil. She had a schedule mapped out, one that would remind everyone of Santa, and would help all the charitable organizations Claus & Company had set up to deal with the other problems that the public noticed only at Christmas—poverty, homelessness, starvation (even in big countries like the US), and childhood illnesses. She loved using her position at Claus & Company to goose holiday donations.

She didn't want to be distracted from that mission.

And if anyone would distract, it would be a voice-voice. Palmer's was perfect. That quintessential American announcer combination between kind, reassuring, and authoritative. Palmer sounded like an adult version of your very best friend.

Nissa frowned at the entire idea of it.

"This Palmer is on a mission against what exactly?" she asked. "Santa?"

"No, no," Oskar said as if that were unthinkable, and

it probably was. "Professor Palmer is on an anti-obesity mission, and that's a bandwagon that everyone seems to be jumping on of late. But he has a particularly interesting way of approaching it. He says we shouldn't be tolerant of role models who overindulge."

"That's not original." Nissa had heard that argument since she left the Pole and moved to New York, almost two decades ago. "And besides, criticizing role models doesn't work. America hates judgmental types."

Oskar patted his shirt pocket. She realized he was looking for a cigarette. From across the table, someone slid him a cigarette package. With a camel on the cover.

She didn't know if someone had magicked it as a screw-you to Professor Palmer, or if no one in the room had noticed that the man had even been talking about cigarettes.

"That's the point," Oskar said as he picked up the package. "Somehow this Professor Palmer isn't coming across judgmental. He's managing to come across like a reasonable guy with the solution."

She had no idea how that argument, even made with a voice-voice, could be anything but judgmental. "His solution is to make Santa skinny?"

"No," Oskar said. "The solution is to change Santa's habits. Palmer's arguing that Santa's behavior is very last century, and we need a new Santa for the modern age."

She looked at Oskar in surprise. He was staring at the

blank television, turning the cigarette pack over and over in his hands.

"Do you think he's correct?" she asked.

Oskar shrugged. She couldn't tell if he was being noncommittal or if he did not want to agree with Palmer in front of the Image Specialists.

Still, she wasn't going to let Oskar off the hook.

"You were the one who made Santa's image public," she said. "It's not even really an 'image.' It's who he is. We can't change who he is from the outside."

That had been part of Oskar's genius. He had convinced the mortals in the Greater World that they had created Santa in their own image. In reality, their images just reflected the S-Elf who occupied the position.

Santa got voted in by S-Elves, just like popes got elected in the Catholic Church—only at the North Pole, the vote came a lot less often. Santas held their position for centuries, and could sometimes decree that a beloved child or heir take their place. It all depended on the S-Elf's magical capability, purity of his elf heritage, his empathy, and his political skills.

"You're not saying we're getting a new Santa, are you?" she asked, feeling both alarmed and intrigued. She'd been hearing rumors for years now that the current Santa was getting tired and wanted to pick a successor soon. She hoped that a female S-Elf would get the position, but had been informed that such a thing would never occur in her lifetime. Every century of it.

"No, I'm not saying Santa's retiring," Oskar said as one of the women slapped the television. It vibrated on its stand. Nissa wanted to tell the woman that hitting a television to make the picture clear hadn't worked in more than fifty years, but she knew she was just wasting her breath.

"Then what are you saying?" Nissa asked.

"There are a lot of competing images out there," Oskar said. "Lots of things that demand the modern child's attention. Santa is one of the few pure things left. For about ten years, a child gets to believe that magic exists. So many then get over that, and their lives become dull and sad. But those that hang on to the spark—"

"Yes, yes, I know," she said. She wanted him to get to the point. Everyone in the North Pole had been raised on this ideology. Those children who hang on to the spark become the Greater World's optimists, the ones who believe anything is possible if they only give it a try. The others, well, life got increasingly more dreary for them as the years progressed.

She'd never seen any studies that proved or disproved this theory, but that didn't change the fact that everyone in the Pole used the theory as an argument. And honestly, she loved that theory. It was one reason she worked for Image Headquarters at Claus & Company. To use Santa's good image to promote everything she cared about.

But her desire to get to the point got misinterpreted.

"Don't dismiss that idea, missy," said Ludwig, who sat in the back. He was one of the oldest of the Old Boys, a man with a long white beard, a subservient wife, and an ego the size of the Atlantic Ocean. She had always wondered how he'd managed to keep that ego in check so he could work with Oskar.

The other Old Boys also had egos, just not as big as Ludwig's or Oskar's. They all had had illustrious careers, careers she'd studied in Image class, and then confirmed (in her own way) on her days off in New York. She'd spent a lot of time in the New York Public Library, digging through old images and archives, looking for pictures of the Old Boys.

And she'd found a few, mostly in group settings like this one, holding stogies and some kind of liquor and looking very pleased with themselves.

"I'm not dismissing the argument," she said, trying not to sound defensive, even though she *had* been trying to move Oskar forward. She wanted out of this room. "I'm just familiar with it. We all are. I understand how important child-magic-beliefs are."

She probably shouldn't snap at her so-called betters. Not if she wanted to remain employed.

And while she found a lot to dislike about life in the North Pole, working for Claus & Company was one of the best jobs in any world, Greater or otherwise. She wasn't sure what would happen to her if she got fired. She wasn't even sure if she could continue to live in New York. She might have to come back here and work the toy-manufacturing line—the physical line, not the one that used magic. Her magic wasn't strong enough to work on the magic part of toy assembly. She'd learned that early. As a young mage, she'd put in her time at the physical assembly line. Even now, the idea of putting safe, plastic baby toys in gift-wrapped boxes made her shiver.

"Well, then, missy," said Ludwig. "Shape up your attitude."

She started to take a deep breath to calm herself, then changed her mind, and exhaled. She would make it through this meeting without coughing. She *would*.

Oskar looked at her sideways, with just a bit of sympathy. Then he patted her knee. His hand came to rest on her thigh. She wanted to tell him that such familiarity wouldn't play in the Greater World, but she knew what he'd say. This wasn't the Greater World.

He'd say this was better.

And he might be right.

She frowned at the blank television. Professor Palmer droned on. Although really, she couldn't call his side of the conversation droning. Even without the visuals, he was compelling. He had to have some magic. Or supreme amounts of charisma. It wasn't just the argument alone that made him impossible to ignore.

"I'm still not clear on any of this," she said. "What does this Palmer want, exactly?"

"He wants Santa to be a force for good," Oskar said.

Well, *that* was offensive. "Santa *is* a force for good," she said.

If she didn't believe that, she wouldn't be working for Claus & Company. She wouldn't have given up her life for it.

"We know that," Oskar said, "but Professor Palmer's tarnishing the brand. We can't allow that. We must control the image ourselves."

She looked at Oskar's sincere, unlined face, and resisted the urge to remove his hand from her thigh. She didn't want to offend him, although really, Palmer and the job he represented was annoying her.

"Can't we just let this blow over?" she asked Oskar.

"Some things blow over, some things don't," Oskar said.

She'd heard that before as well. It was Marketing 101. The next thing he'd say would be that if they didn't get ahead of this train, then it would pass them by, and she would say that if they got in front of a train, it could run them over, and then they'd all argue about the use of metaphor and whether or not it was accurate, and then they'd return to the topic, and the decision would end up being the same.

When Oskar had an idea this strong, no one crossed him.

But she had to try. "I'm afraid if we give this professor credence, then the story will become bigger."

"...not even sure kids can relate to Santa anymore," Palmer was saying. "One hundred years ago, a fat, sated man was the epitome of wealth. Now we know that such a man is a heart attack waiting to happen. We associate his level of obesity with a lack of care instead of too much care..."

She closed her eyes. Okay. *That* was a good argument. Santa the Slovenly was not going to play in Peoria.

Oskar's hand slid a little too close to her inner thigh. He leaned over and blew cigarette breath on her. "*Now* do you understand?"

"Yeah," she said, opening her eyes. The television image had returned, and it now showed rows and rows of clapping people, all looking pleased. "Unfortunately, I do."

Visions of Sugar Plums

CHAPTER TWO

RYAN PALMER SPIT the last of the mouthwash into the highball glass and replaced the plastic lid. Then he opened the little cupboard on the limo's side door and placed the entire mess in the dirty-dish box. That he knew where this model of limo stashed its dirty dishes pointed to the fact that he had spent too much of the last few weeks doing press interviews on someone else's dime, and not enough time actually living his life.

And now he was in New York. He'd recognize the city just from its sound. Honking horns, construction noise, the rush of traffic—all audible through the limo's sound-proof windows. He loved the city. He'd gone to school here. At any other point, he would look out the window, compare the city now to the days when he had lived here, but not even that interested him. Right now, all he wanted to do was get to his hotel and take a very long nap.

Which wouldn't happen for at least three hours, maybe more.

The limo had pulled up in the elite section of the underground parking at one of the most famous network buildings in America. They even had had three television shows named after this place's *address*. So many famous people went in and out of here that they needed several protected entrances, even though it was New York, and all the locals were supposedly blasé about the famous.

Ryan did not want to be here yet. All the way from the airport, he'd been angling to be let off at his hotel. He figured he had an hour before he had to arrive for whatever show was on his schedule next, an hour in which he could shower, put on different clothes, and maybe, just maybe, be alone for just a few minutes.

Ryan had asked the driver to take him to the hotel and the driver had politely refused. After all, Ryan hadn't hired the driver, and drivers hired by publicists knew better than to drop an unsupervised client at an unplanned location. That was how drivers got fired and unsupervised clients made it into the tabloids.

Although Ryan didn't think he was famous enough to be tabloid fodder. *Yet*, his publicist would say. Or rather, the publicist hired by the university would say. That publicist came highly recommended, from the university's usual PR firm. The firm's usual university publicists handled the athletic department—the young kids who had no idea how to play Famous Star Quarterback or Nearly Superstar Basketball Player, not to mention the coaches and assistants who generally put a foot in something (and not always their mouths).

No, that firm wasn't used to a mild-mannered scientist who specialized in public health. In fact, upon meeting him, the publicist had told him that everything about his resume screamed *Stay Away From the Media!* Her name was Wendy ("Think magic!" she said when she introduced herself. "You know, like Peter Pan."), and she was younger than half his students, although infinitely more focused.

If it hadn't been for the YouTube video one of his graduate assistants had talked him into making, Ryan wouldn't be "on the cutting edge of celebrity," as Wendy said, speaking learnedly about something that everyone else was taking just a tad too seriously.

Ryan could not believe the fuss. Santa Claus did not exist, except in the imaginations of small children. Santa Claus in the 21st century was a media creation that the people once known as the Wizards of Madison Avenue had created to sell cola, for heaven's sake.

Back in the days when cola had cocaine in it.

The limo driver opened the door, startling Ryan. "We're here, Doctor Palmer."

Ryan hated being called "doctor," too. He had a medical degree, but he chose not to use it. He never really trusted himself with diagnosis, and he had discovered that he hated surgery. He preferred "Professor," but no one in this weird media realm he found himself in wanted to use that.

Actually, he suspected Wendy told them not to. She thought "doctor" was a lot more impressive and added to his credibility.

Think Doctor Phil, she said.

Indeed, Ryan had replied, who was thinking of Dr. Phil, a man with a Ph.D., but no medical license. Ryan hadn't said anything disparaging, but only because he had learned that arguing with Wendy was like arguing with his C students about homework—there really was no point.

"I'm told they got clothes for you upstairs. Someone will meet you at the door and get you to makeup," the driver said.

Oh, goodie, Ryan thought, but didn't add. Because really, who said "goodie," any more anyway, at least as a full-fledged adult.

"Thank you," he said, and reached for his wallet. He was going to tip this driver, no matter what anyone said. This guy had at least been friendly.

"No, no," the driver said, waving his meaty hands. "I get well paid by your company. I'm not allowed to do the tip thing."

He didn't even sound regretful, unlike the driver in LA who had complained about that regulation for half the drive through the virtual city that was LAX. There, Ryan had been happy to raise the privacy screen.

He got out of the limo into a semi-decorated parking garage filled with murals of famous faces. That still didn't get rid of the stench of exhaust and spilled beer, but it did let him know he was in a better class of parking structure.

As if that mattered.

He got onto the elevator and closed his eyes as the door eased shut. Just a moment of alone-time, but that moment might mean everything. When this little whirlwind was over, he was going to get off the media merry-go-round; he didn't care how many books it sold or how famous he got. He didn't want to be Dr. Palmer, talking about children's health on national television and listening to fat people complain that their holiday recipes were a once-per-year indulgence and a family tradition.

A slender arm with red nails and pricy bangles caught the door just before it closed. He felt a second of irritation before the door slid back to reveal the woman of his dreams.

This woman was tall and slender, with wedge-cut black hair and almond-shaped black eyes that snapped with intelligence. Her mouth was thin and a shade of red that matched those nails. But the rest of her makeup was subtle: pre-television makeup, the kind that kept the beautiful beautiful before they became HD-ready.

She wore a form-fitting black dress that suggested but didn't quite execute an art deco design. The dress's geometric patterns actually accented the wedges in the woman's hair. She clutched a white wool coat to her chest, as if she were hot (and she *was* hot, just not that kind of hot), even though it had to be below freezing in the elevator itself. She wore strappy, high-heel shoes that made her as tall as he was, and some kind of silvery legging that suggested both nylons and leg warmers.

He had noticed all of that as she made her way across the elevator's tiny space. He was staring, and that was probably wrong. Besides, identifying her as the woman of his dreams just proved that he was exhausted. He didn't have dreams about women—except those dreams that he assumed every man had (and enjoyed) in those long days between relationships.

She nodded at him, and then did the urban-elevator gaze. It focused on the changing numbers, as the elevator climbed its way up. He was heading to the third floor. He figured a woman clutching a large tote bag, a heavy wool coat, and the latest, coolest tablet would be going up higher in this seventy-story building, maybe to one of the business floors.

Her hair moved ever so slightly revealing a small ear. It looked vaguely pointed, which, for some geeky reason, made her even more attractive to him.

He sighed, and that made her glance directly at him. He gave her a nervous smile—he was always nervous around beautiful women—and then he focused on the elevator's crawling numbers just like she did.

Finally, after what felt like two hundred years, a *ping* announced their arrival on the third floor. He shifted as the door opened, then watched in surprise as she stepped out first. He had almost impolitely shoved his way past her, assuming she was getting out on a different floor, and he was glad he hadn't. For some reason, he didn't want to seem rude in the eyes of a woman he had never really met and would probably never see again.

Wendy, darling Wendy, Wendy darling, (he sighed a second time) was waiting for him outside the elevator, her own tablet clutched against her massive (and expensively artificial) chest. She resembled a cartoon drawing of a beautiful woman next to the woman who had just gotten off the elevator. Wendy was taller and thinner, but her red hair had an orange tint that looked dyed, despite the efforts of the high-end salon that catered to her every whim.

Wendy was frowning at him and he wondered just how rumpled he looked.

"Who was that?" she asked, glancing at the back of the beautiful woman who was now walking down the hall.

"How should I know?" he answered. That beautiful woman could have been the biggest superstar in the world, and he wouldn't have had the slightest idea who she was. He followed media *trends*, but not industry gossip. He never knew who the latest, hottest star was. He'd learned, following trends as they applied to public health, that what was hot now would be forgotten a few weeks from now.

Except for the mega-trends, the mega-creations like—um—Santa Claus.

"She looks familiar," Wendy said, but not in a positive I-just-saw-someone-famous way, but in a this-could-be-a-disaster way.

Ryan shrugged. He didn't want to think about the beautiful woman any more. Which wasn't exactly true. He did want to think about her. When he conjured up ideas of female beauty. Alone. Not before yet another dumb interview.

"Is there a green room?" he asked, changing the subject.

"You're not going to the green room," Wendy said. "You need a shower, a change of clothes, and makeup. You have shadows under your eyes that children could sleep in."

Wendy, darling Wendy, Wendy darling. She was the one who had set up the brutal press schedule in the first place. Didn't she realize that real humans needed to sleep and eat and maybe sit by themselves at least once every day?

Oh, wait. He had already had that discussion with her, and she had said, *You can handle this for six weeks.* They had known each other maybe an hour at that point, and he had never figured out what made her so certain he could cope with a killer schedule.

Even now, four weeks in, she wouldn't listen when he mentioned sleeping and eating and alone time. She seemed to believe he should get up from the six hours of sleep the brutal schedule allowed him, and look camera-ready.

He wasn't camera-ready on eight-plus hours of sleep, let alone when he was jet-lagged, woozy with exhaustion, and *hungry*. That slice of pizza he'd managed to snag on the way through the airport had held him for exactly 90 minutes.

He said, "Is there food—?"

"There's always food in the green room," she snapped. "Make sure none of it sticks in your teeth."

The green room was one shower, some stupid dress clothes, and a half hour in the makeup chair away from him. His stomach was already rumbling.

If he had known the price of media fame was exhaustion, boredom, and repeating the same argument in front of a new group of (unbelievably dumb) talking heads, he wouldn't have signed on in the first place.

And, to be fair to himself, he'd tried not to sign on. The president of the university had convinced him to do this. *We're in a tough time,* the president had said. *We can't continue raising tuition. We need alumni donations now more than ever, and alumni tend to donate when someone from their alma mater becomes famous for the right things, especially things we can exploit academically. So help us out, Ry, okay?*

That "Ry" had almost made Ryan say no. No one

called him "Ry." He sounded like bread. But he had agreed, because he did care about the university. And he had thought getting his message out would help kids and families.

He hadn't expected everything to focus on the three pages in his book where he had used Santa Claus as an example of harmful media hype that needed updating for the modern era.

"Doctor Palmer?" Wendy said in that tone that he was sure she would use on a poor, defenseless husband someday. "Shall we?"

Ryan sighed a third time. *Once more into the breach,* he thought, because he knew saying it out loud would be worthless. Wendy would ask him what it meant, and then he'd have to explain *Henry the Fifth*. Hell, he might have to explain Shakespeare.

Wendy was a high-end representative of the media/publicity/punditry class. She was smarter than most, which wasn't saying much.

He'd been on a few shows where he felt like he'd have to explain who Santa Claus was.

He hoped the upcoming appearance wasn't one of those.

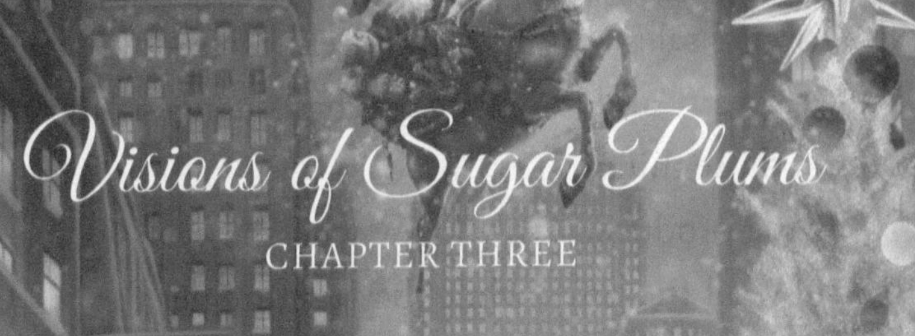

Visions of Sugar Plums

CHAPTER THREE

T HE MAN IN the elevator had been unbelievably gorgeous. Magically gorgeous. So gorgeous, in fact, that Nissa worried he was a celebrity whom she didn't recognize. She'd met a lot of celebrities who could make themselves look relatively normal with the right choice of clothes, stubble, and a two-day lack of sleep. She used the word relatively, because it was always hard to hide the great facial architecture that a camera loved, blue eyes that suggested a thousand perfect summer days, and lips so kissable that it was hard for a woman—any woman—to resist.

Get a grip, she told herself as she headed down the hall to check in with the producers of the show she privately called *Made-up Controversies Are Us*. She'd been on the show dozens of times, usually in the holiday season. But she'd become a regular at other times of year, talking about retail sales and unemployment rates—only because she was pretty and articulate and had a tangential connection to those things.

If the producers truly knew who she was, she'd be on the show all the time, while they tried to get the Big Guy as the Big Get. But she used her time to plug Claus & Company, and then to remind people to donate to whatever cause was at the top of the company list that week.

Besides, she liked being the go-to girl when the producers needed something. That meant she could trade favor for favor, and get on the show when she really needed to.

She really needed to this time. She needed to deal with that Palmer idiot before he got any more airtime. She had promised the producers excellent television, so she needed to be focusing on her arguments.

Not on that incredibly handsome man in the elevator.

That was the weird thing: She saw incredibly handsome men all the time. She worked in PR, for heaven's sake, and she was on television daily during the holiday season. When she came to this place, the home of two networks (one a spin-off) spread out over a dozen floors, she saw Everyone Who Was Anyone. The big names were either doing talk shows or long-running variety shows, always here to promote their latest TV series/album/film.

She had shared a table with George Clooney in the commissary and not lost her head over his gorgeousness.

(Honestly, in real life, he was a bit too thin—just like most actors. Not because they hated food, but because of that camera-ready thing.)

She had corralled one of Brad Pitt's 800 children, who, Pitt assured her when she brought the kid into the green room, was usually better behaved. She went out onto the loading dock one afternoon and stumbled on Ewan McGregor, smoking. She had been a bit stunned at just how short he was.

The thing about actors, producers, writers, *celebrities*, was that they were real people and yeah, they might be good on TV or gorgeously airbrushed in the pages of *Vanity Fair*, but they had a human side just like everyone else. They wore too much cologne or ate with their mouths open or fell asleep and snored in the makeup chair.

Even though she'd met almost all of *People Magazine's* Sexiest Man Alive honorees (if you wanted to call them that), none of them had hijacked her brain (and other parts) quite like Elevator Guy.

She probably should call him something else in her head. Or at least, try to forget him. Because she hadn't even heard him speak. She hadn't quite brought herself to say hello.

If, by chance, he was some celebrity she didn't recognize, then she would seem like Creepy Stalker Fan Girl, and that would make her horribly unprofessional. Right now, on this stupid mission from the North Pole, she *felt* unprofessional, so she didn't need to do anything to reinforce that sense of herself.

She waved at the receptionist when she reached the part of the floor dedicated to the show. "Can I go in?" Nissa asked, and then proceeded to walk to the back without waiting for an answer. The mark of a permanent guest; no one stopped her when she walked past reception.

Behind the public areas, the halls were narrow, painted a dirty eggshell, and blocked by boxes and other things some intern needed to take care of three weeks ago. She let herself into a relatively large (by New York standards) office overlooking the plaza and its fountain. Tourists milled, hoping they could see celebrities or get into free show tapings, while New Yorkers picked their way past with expressions of great annoyance. She could empathize.

The city always got crowded during the holiday season —particularly in this part, near the skating rink and the big Christmas tree and Radio City Music Hall, all those things Flyover Country had heard about since the Christmas movies of the 1940s.

Caryn Longworth, the executive producer, sat behind her desk. She had a horsey, not-camera-ready face filled with intelligence so overpowering that one look in her eyes was terrifying. According to staff gossip, Caryn was related to at least two former US Presidents, several senators, and one famous hostess from the days when women didn't serve in Congress. Caryn had the familial political brains, a rabid enthusiasm for government gossip, and a fine-tuned sense of news-as-entertainment.

Nissa loved her. They often went out for coffee together to discuss the day's TV highlights. They weren't quite best friends—neither of them felt like they were in the position to have best friends—but they would have been if they'd had different jobs.

"Please tell me this idiot professor has canceled," Nissa said to Caryn.

"Oh, Nissie hasn't done her homework," Caryn said with a twinkle that rivaled the Big Guy's. "Our professor is not an idiot by a long stretch."

"I've done enough homework to know that," Nissa said, although she hadn't been able to download any of the shows he'd appeared on. She hadn't had enough time.

"But apparently you haven't seen enough to realize that you better bring your A game," Caryn said seriously.

Nissa felt a half second of panic. Caryn had never said that to her. Caryn, in fact, said that Nissa's B game was better than everyone else's A game.

Caryn was, in some ways, her biggest fan.

"He's here then," Nissa said, pretending to misunderstand her friend.

"Oh, he's here, along with his brilliance, his beauty, and his stellar Q rating."

"What?" Nissa asked. "He has a Q Score?"

The Q Score was a metric that TV people in particular used to keep track of someone's appeal to a particular audience. Personalities with high Q Scores got more invitations to appear on television than people with no Q Scores.

Santa had a Q Score as a brand and a cartoon figure, but not as a personality. Nissa had a Q Score as a personality and it was pretty good for someone with no actual video venue of her own.

"Our professor does have a Q Score," Caryn said. "He had one *before* he ever went on TV."

"How is that possible?" Nissa asked.

"One of the most popular YouTube videos of all time," Caryn said. "You really haven't done your homework on this one."

Nissa felt her cheeks heat. "I just got assigned this yesterday," she said. "And then I was away from any internet connection. I thought he was just some anti-Santa guy."

"That's what makes him great," Caryn said. "He sounds so *pro*-Santa while being against everything that Santa does. He sounds like Dr. Oz or somebody, totally concerned with your health while basically saying you're stupid just for breathing."

"Great," Nissa said under her breath. "Too bad Santa can't rebut him."

Santa would destroy him. Charm, charisma, the ability to make someone believe that even the silliest things were possible—that was the true magic of an S-Elf.

If only Nissa could get Santa here for one media appearance.

Although, she knew, that would be completely impossible.

"Yes, it is too bad that Santa can't rebut him," Caryn said. "But you'd need Edmund Gwenn for that, wouldn't you? And he's been dead since what? The 1950s?"

Nissa frowned at her, thinking for a moment before understanding the reference. Edmund Gwenn had played Kris Kringle in the original movie version of *Miracle on 34th Street*. There was quite a back story to the performance. The entire movie existed because of Oskar. Oskar put a bug in the ear of somebody at Twentieth Century Fox to do a movie about the possibility of Santa being real. The movie was having difficulties until, in a very Ghost of Christmas Present maneuver, Oskar took Gwenn to the North Pole to meet the real Santa, all the while letting Gwenn think he dreamed the whole thing.

Santa nearly blew it all by showing up at the Oscars while on vacation. When Gwenn won for his performance, Santa had shaken his hand on the way up to the stage. *Now I know there is a Santa Claus!* Gwenn exclaimed when he won, and everyone thought he meant that he was referring to the award, when actually, he was referring to the Jolly Old Elf who had just shaken his hand.

"Nissa?" Caryn asked.

"Sorry," Nissa said. "Wool-gathering."

"Well, you shouldn't," Caryn said. "You should use that fancy tablet of yours to watch what you're up against. This guy is disarming, and he's funny, and one of the sexiest guests we've had."

"It's not hard to get that appellation on this show," Nissa said, referring to the fact that most guests on *Made-up Controversies Are Us* were on the political side and therefore were not incredibly attractive by TV standards.

"Still," Caryn said. "You've got less than an hour to prepare."

"You just want good TV," Nissa said.

"Damn straight," Caryn said, "and I'm afraid this guy's going to eat you for lunch."

The
Santa
SERIES

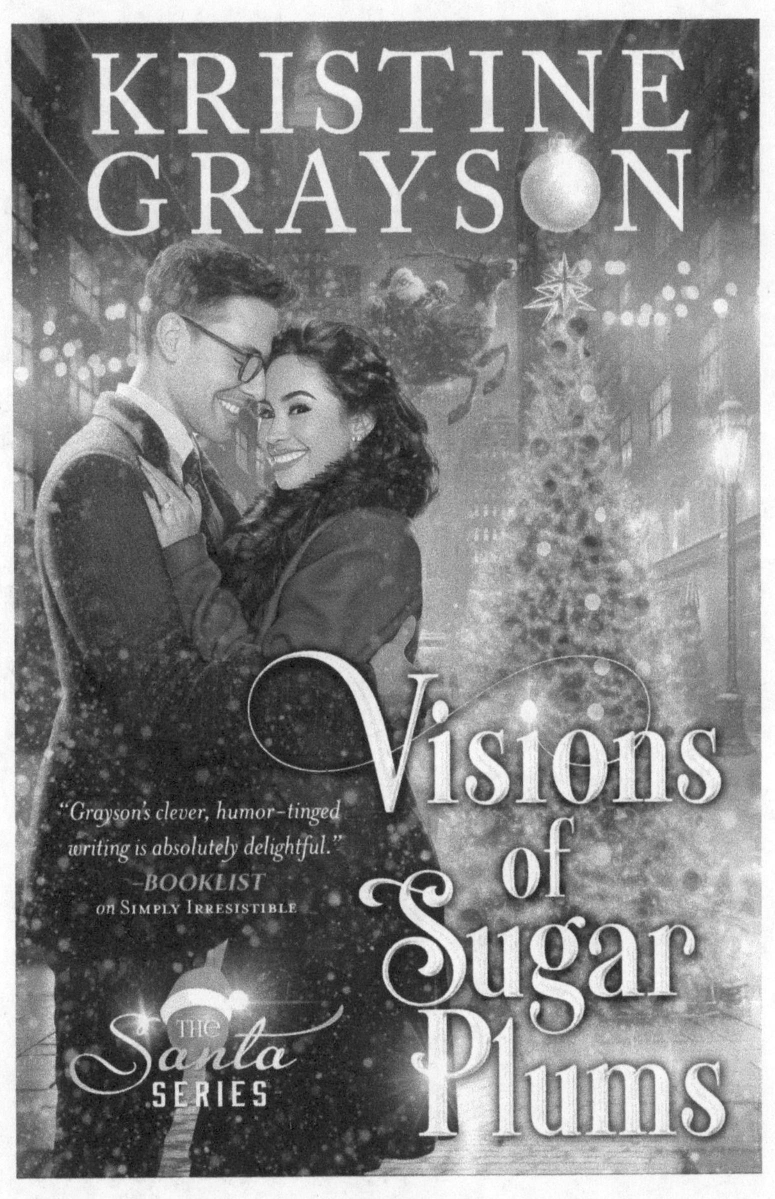

Keep Reading *Visions of Sugar Plums!*

Go to WMGbooks.com

But Wait, There's More!

Want more holiday goodies?

Go to wmgholidayspectacular.com.

Hear Directly From Kris!

Keep up with the latest news, releases and so much more
—even the occasional giveaway!

To sign up for the Kristine Grayson newsletter, a pen
name of Kristine Kathryn Rusch, **go to kriswrites.com.**

You can also **follow Kris on Bookbub.**

Get the latest news and releases from all of WMG's authors and lines, including Kristine Kathryn Rusch, Dean Wesley Smith, *Pulphouse Magazine*, and more...

To sign up, **go to wmgbooks.com**.

Called "The Reigning Queen of Paranormal Romance" by Best Reviews, bestselling author Kristine Grayson (also known by her real name, Kristine Kathryn Rusch) has made a name for herself publishing light, slightly off-skew romance novels about Greek Gods, fairy tale characters, and the modern world.

Her novel Utterly Charming, won the Romantic Times Reviewer's Choice Award for Best Contemporary Paranormal Romance.

She writes in several series, including the Fates Series, the Charming Series, and the Santa Series.

Her Daughters of Zeus Trilogy is YA set in the same skewed universe, and she writes Middle Grade stories about the daughters of Cinderella and Prince Charming.

As Kristine Grayson, she also edits the romance volumes of Fiction River: An Original Anthology Magazine.

For more information about her work, go to kriswrites.com and sign up for the Kristine Grayson newsletter.